JOHN THE OLD SAXON

KING ALFRED AND THE REVIVAL OF ANGLO-SAXON LEARNING

JOHN BROUGHTON

In finem· Psalmus David
Exaudiat te dominus in die
tribulationis; protegat te nomen
dei Iacob. Mittat tibi auxilium
de sancto et de Sion tueatur te.
Memor sit omnis sacrificii tui et
holocaustum tuum pingue fiat

Frontispiece: Interpretation of Brother Asher's illustration of Psalm 20
by Dawn Burgoyne.

This book is dedicated to the memory of Arthur Broughton, (1898-1956) my grandfather, who instilled in me a love of history, but was lost to me far too soon.

FOREWORD

"There follow in order the Reudignians, and Aviones, and Angles and Varinians, and Eudoses, and Suardones, and Nuithones; all defended by rivers or forests. Nor in one of these nations does aught remarkable occur, only that they universally join in the worship of *Herthum* (*Nerthus*) that is to say, the Mother Earth." —Tacitus, 'Germania'

PREFACE

Athelney Abbey, Wessex 904 AD

This tale is not about me, but about my beloved friend, flown to the bosom of our Saviour at a ripe old age earlier this year. My given name is Asher, like the eighth son of Jacob, but I am known here in my adopted land as Gwyn, meaning *Blessed*. I am a stranger from a land stranger still. Born in Old Saxony— I use the term to distinguish my homeland from that of Seaxna or New Saxony, whose people I frequent on these Britannic shores—I am the grandson of an illustrious grandfather, and must recount whence my friend John and I came.

Consider the shape of a triangle. Well, that was my homeland. From angle to angle a man would travel for eight days. The greatest of the tribal duchies, Old Saxony, embraced the whole territory between the lower Elbe and the Saale rivers almost as far as the wide Rhine. Between the mouths of the Elbe and the Weser, it bordered the North Sea. Ay, that devourer of ships, which our folk crossed at their peril many years ago to settle in the green and pleasant land where I now reside. I remain proud of my origins.

Our lands were a broad plain, save on the south, where they rose into hills and the low mountainous country of the Harz and Hesse. This low divide was all that separated our country of the Saxons from our ancient enemies and ultimate conquerors, the Franks.

That is why I admire my grandfather. His name was Widukind, which means *child of the woods*. His reluctance to accept the new Christian religion and propensity to mount destructive raids on our neighbours brought him into direct conflict with Charlemagne, the powerful king of the Franks and, later, emperor. After a bloody and attritional thirty-year campaign between 772–804, the Old Saxons led by my grandfather were eventually subdued by Charlemagne and even he was forced to convert to Christianity.

His life alone is worth a book and, maybe one day, I will use my scribing skills to revere him if my arthritic fingers, getting no younger, will permit. But first, they must toil over this vellum to honour the life of my old friend, John. His was one of the sharpest minds of his generation. Also, his learning surpassed that of any man I have ever known. Yet, in his youth, he was a fearsome warrior and it is in those years in Old Saxony that his tale must begin.

ONE

I am an old man and can no longer hold the quill in my arthritic fingers. So, I have enlisted a young scribe, Brother Otmar, to set down my words. The youth has a keen mind and a steady hand. Also, he is of kindly disposition, only too eager to help this aged monk. All that is required is to rack my memory, for I will refer to a time more than a lifetime ago.

Gandersheim, Old Saxony, 830 AD

I will try to remember my first conversation with John word for word. We lay on an ice-cold flagged floor in a dungeon, close around our ankle an iron band chained to a ring in a damp stone wall, dripping rivulets of water. Defeated, captured, I was flogged and flung into the grim depths of a Frankish castle along with eight of my comrades.

"Don't worry, we'll soon be out of here," were John's first improbable words to me. I must have given him an evil glare because he hissed, "Suit yourself, but I'm telling you—"

"What?" I snarled, "that these chains will shed themselves and the guards will let us go, perhaps with a flask of wine in our

1

hands?" He seemed impervious to the sarcasm and impatience of a twenty-year-old.

"I was saying, my family will have us released any day now."

"Either that or they'll bind us to a tree and riddle us with arrows."

The truth is, I blamed him and his damned way with words for our plight. If he hadn't stirred the sleeping wolf in our breasts, preying on our festering resentment of the Franks, we would have been out free to breathe fresh air, likely tilling our fields. The bonds of kindred and clan are strong among the Saxons, and notwithstanding our many divisions, he found a way to make us unite and revolt. We were of the same age. If I try hard, I can recall his words ringing in my ears on the fateful day I agreed to join him.

"Never forget the Blood Court of Verden, brothers, after Widukind defeated a Frankish army at the Battle of Suntel. What did Charlemagne do? You all know! He ordered the beheading of 4500 rebel Saxons on a single day. Let us fight to avenge them!"

Nobody cheered louder than I. He could not have known about the family connection but he had referred to my grand-sire and a massacre that occurred forty-eight years before, during the Saxon Wars. The prisoner lying next to me was a Christian, but he artfully roused the wolf by reminding our folk of Charlemagne's edict *Capitulatio de partibus Saxoniae* which asserted, *If any one of the race of the Saxons hereafter concealed among them shall have wished to hide himself unbaptized, and shall have scorned to come to baptism and shall have wished to remain a pagan, let him be punished by death.* Lying on that pitiless, cold stone floor, lashing out with bare feet at intrepid rats approaching their unprotected toes, each one of our other companions secretly worshipped Woden.

John should have known that the Franks were better armed and organised than the ill-disciplined but courageous rebels he had mustered. His stirring speeches tugged at the hearts and minds of our oppressed folk. He spoke of a glorious opportunity because, not for the first time, our count, Wala, was aiding Lothair I, the eldest son of Louis the Pious, in rebellion against his father. In that May, 830, a short-lived uprising involving those of both clerical and lay orders as well as three elder sons of Louis, succeeded in forcing Empress Judith into monastic confinement. John declared this the perfect chance to over-throw the Franks. It might have been, had the rebellion lasted longer. As it was, the rebels managed to put pressure on Louis the Pious to abdicate. But their success was not enduring, for Wala finished in exile in a high mountainous region near Lake Geneva. With the undivided attention of the Franks in Saxony given to our uprising, our hopes were dashed on the battlefield.

I must admit that the tall, muscular figure lying beside me fought ferociously. I had wielded my axe close enough to him to admire the slaughter he effected. If all of our warriors had been so valiant, we would have carried the day. John only surren-dered when the remnants of our force were surrounded by a ring of spearmen. Give him his due, he called out in a ringing voice to lay down our arms. Thanks to his discretion that day, I have reached this ripe old age.

Only in that dungeon did we get to talking where he confided that he was the black sheep of his family. The youngest of four children, his eldest brother was the same Wala who had rebelled against the emperor. His father Egbert was a count at the Frankish court, where John had grown up and studied before rebelling and running away, refusing to take monastic vows like his two brothers. His youthful dream, quashed in that dungeon, was to become a warrior and liberate Old Saxony. With hindsight, we were laughably idealistic hot-

3

headed youths back then. And both were sons of a noble family. Perhaps that is why we became lifelong friends.

As I am a venerable monk, I should spare a word about John's mother, Ida of Herzfeld. I would say that it was thanks to her influence that John grew into the man we came to respect and admire. She was the daughter of a count close to Charlemagne and received her education at his court. He gave her in marriage to a favourite lord, Egbert, and bestowed on her a great fortune in estates to recompense her father's services. She was a saintly woman who devoted her life to the poor following the death of her husband in 811. But I am getting ahead of myself. I will return to Ida later in my narrative.

Two days after my first exchange with John, his words came true. Despite my scepticism, we were bundled outdoors and menaced in the courtyard.

"We're going for a country stroll," the officer jested, but there was no humour in his next words. "On our journey, if any man is stupid enough to run away, he will be caught. In that case"—there was an evil glint in his eye—"he'll lose a foot. I'll chop it off myself! Clear?" He bellowed, repeating the question and waving an axe. None of us doubted the sincerity of his threat.

They handed back our shoes. "You'll be needing these," and even this sounded ominous. Six and a half days of torture began as we jogged along on the trot whilst our captors, brandishing canes to discourage laggards, rode beside us. Only our thin linen protected us from those stinging wands. The weaker among us wore shirts dappled with bloodstains. "No cheese for malingerers!" the Frank bawled with gusto. That admonition kept us on our toes. We needed the hard, black rye bread and the rocklike goat's cheese to replenish our dwindling energy, but it was water we craved most. Six leagues a day, due south, they required of us. Whence and to what fate was not revealed.

After six and a half days, we arrived at our destination, although we knew it not. I had admired the beauty of the wood-lands fringing the broad swirling river, which later I learnt was the Fulda. The monastery, founded a little more than half a century before, lay before us.

"Your new home, brothers," sneered the officer. "The Duke has given you a choice: either become monks or die. What is it to be? Those among you not wishing to wear the habit, step forward now!" Unsurprisingly, nobody moved a tired muscle to advance. "Right! Prepare to be tonsured." They made us kneel, tugged at our hair and carved it away with their daggers. It hurt like hell and I'm convinced they relished nicking as many scalps as possible.

When his tormentor had finished, John, knelt next to me, muttered, "This is my father's doing, I'll wager. He always wanted me to be a monk, like my brothers."

"Better a monk than a corpse," I whispered back, running my hand over my sore head. The soldier had done a poor job with his knife. I felt the stubble against my palm. "Maybe the brothers will supply us with razors," I said—correctly, as it turned out. We dragged our aching bones through the monastery gates and admired the stone buildings we grew to know and love. The abbey had everything necessary for monastic life. Looking back, the founder, Sturm, had chosen a magnificent remote location amid luxuriant surroundings. Yet, inside the walls nothing was lacking, the facilities included workshops for a variety of trades, stables, pigsties, pens, beehives, a smithy, furnaces, ovens and, of course, a chapel.

We were greeted by a prior, whose first action was to send for the infirmarian, which was the measure of this kindly monk. He had spied the blood-soaked linen on our backs and called for a soothing balm to treat the raw wheals. His second action was to enquire who among us could read and write. The only man to raise his hand stood next to me: my friend, John. The day had not passed before they put him to the test to demonstrate how learned and refined he was. It ensured his entry to the scriptorium, which proved to be a formative experience for him, whereas they consigned me to the chandler to learn the craft of candle-making.

The irony of our forced march of forty leagues, I discovered later, was that the place we had departed from, Gandersheim, was soon destined to have a monastery or, rather, a convent. On reflection, none of our motley crew would have graced a nunnery!

Within the first year, only one of our band left the monastery, for we were happy there. Fulda provided everything a man might need in exchange for service and dedication to prayer. I am pleased to think that we each grew into worthy brothers in Christ. Except, as I said, for one, a certain Gangolf who did not leave of his free will, but was banished for persistent petty thievery. He was likely destined to die in abject poverty in some squalid and ill-famed quarter. I know that Brother Irmgard had a secret hankering to worship Woden, but he wisely kept his sinful desires to himself. I caught him giving pieces of bread to a crow he frequented too often, but I never remarked on the sacred bird, contenting myself with a wry smile. However, I must not ramble and will, instead, relate something of John's life at Fulda.

TWO

On the day we tramped into the monastery, I noticed the large number of beehives set apart from the monastic buildings. A passing glance cannot reveal the industrious work of the bees and the beekeeper in the apiary. When assigned to the chandlery, for no evident reason except that I could not read or write proficiently, I had no knowledge or interest in the candle-making trade. Soon, I came to change my attitude. The candle-maker has a glorious but difficult occupation. Although my book is about John, it would be remiss of me not to detail how our divergent courses came to run together. The Fulda chandlery is as good a place as any to start that narrative.

My lot was to sweat over vats of molten wax, which was uncomfortable on hot summer days but blissful during the January snows. When I took in the aroma of beeswax, I breathed the flowers and grasses visited by the bees, the monks who tend the herb garden, the folk who hay the fields and the fruit growers who prune the orchards. We bring the land into our sanctuary in the form of altar candles. I still recall the joy of self-realisation at my first Easter in Fulda. We sang the *Exultet* at the Vigil when each person lit his taper, made by me, from the Paschal Candle, made by the chandler.

When I strolled over to chat with the brother beekeeper, I discovered to my surprise that he obtained two pounds of wax for each hundred pounds of honey. He explained this to me as he rinsed and drained the cappings in warm water. Satisfied, he threw them into a double-boiler to melt the wax; at last, I knew how he produced the forty-pound, square blocks that he brought me in his wheelbarrow. These, I liquefied in our fifty-gallon vat, and into the molten mass I repeatedly dipped my wick frame where the cotton wicking became coated by thin layer after layer of wax. After fourteen dippings, the tapers were thick enough and whilst still warm, I cut them out of the surround, trimmed the wicks, and chopped the ends square— all done! When not using a frame for important ceremonial candles, we had moulds where we carefully poured in the molten product. In a few special cases, the chandler trans-formed himself into an artist, shaping wax designs such as flowers or crosses, to colour the plain yellow-white candle shaft. Maybe watching this changed my direction, giving me a craving for creativity, reinforced also by our conversations about John's work. These factors combined to lead me to join John in the scriptorium.

His enthusiastic accounts of new styles coming from Frankia aroused my curiosity, so I took every opportunity to wander into his haven of quills and coloured inks. One day, a striking picture of a kneeling stag in a landscape caught my eye; a red ribbon depicted with a bow tied at the top and bottom of the image. John's deep voice came over my shoulder as I admired it.

"Beautiful, isn't it? It's an evangeliary from Tours in

Frankia. Look, this is just one of the six full-page miniatures. All have ornamental decorations. See here..." He turned the pages. "And here. What do you think of the initials and borders? Aren't they exquisite? Notice how they dyed the parchment purple before writing the gold and silver letters."

"Superb! I wish I could learn to paint such designs."

"Can you even draw?"

I smiled and did not reply. Instead, I bided my time until John was not in the scriptorium. Not wishing to take materials without permission, I spoke with the provisioner, who then indulged me with a few scraps of parchment and allowed me to use a quill and ink at a desk at the back of the room.

Just before I finished my sketch, his curiosity brought him to peer over my shoulder.

"By all the saints, Asher! That is an excellent effort!"

In truth, his words accompanied by laughter were different from those I report here, but bear with me, all will be revealed. That evening, after Compline, I sneaked into the dormer earlier than usual, pulled back John's blanket, and slipped my artwork into his bed. Careful to smooth out the cover as well as my meticulous friend always did, I sat on the edge of mine and waited as the brothers arrived in ones and twos. To appear normal in every respect, I prepared for bed and was cosily under my blanket when John appeared. Unlacing his sandals and stripping to his undergarments, he pulled back the cover and picked up the parchment. Flushed and fighting back laughter he brandished it.

"Who is the scoundrel who did this?"

Curious monks gathered around, peering in the candlelight to grin and point, whispering snide comments.

"My nose is not that big and I do not have hair sprouting from my ears!"

"Oh, yes, you do," I murmured.

He had not heard my remark, but his eyes were boring into mine. Possessed of acute intelligence, he said, "I know whose hand sketched this caricature! *Yours*, Brother Asher, for you are the only one still in bed—the only person not curious to see the drawing. And why is that? Because you knew very well what was on this vellum, did you not?"

Monks were grinning and winking at me.

"I cannot lie. It was I! I wished to prove to you that I can sketch as well as any man here by capturing your *exact* likeness."

He did not rise to the bait but said, "I concede that you have a fine hand, Brother Asher, and everyone present must acknowledge how you captured my handsome features and extraordinary intelligence."

Gales of laughter and ironic applause greeted this statement. One young monk had the temerity to say,

"In truth, Brother John, the sketch is decidedly more handsome than the real person."

This met with gasps followed by much merriment. John glared at the audacious youth, who by no stretch of the imagination would have turned the head of Aphrodite or Persephone, remarked, "Hold your tongue, boy, or I'll have the artist capture your *donkey* features."

"*Eeyore, eeyore!*" several of the brothers brayed, taunting the embarrassed fellow. Everyone went to bed in high good humour.

As the acrid smoke of snuffed candles hung in the dormer air, John's voice from the next bed whispered, "Well done, Asher, I will treasure this gift till the end of my days."

My friends, he kept his word on that score. He also added, "Tomorrow, I will speak with the provisioner and seek to persuade him to let you join us in the scriptorium. Your drawing should convince him."

"Oh, he's already seen it," I whispered back.

"Is there no limit to your knavery?" He pretended to be irate, but I knew him too well.

The next morning, the donkey-featured youth entered the chandlery,

"Brother Asher, the amarius wishes to see you." I had just finished stringing the wicks, so I laid the surround aside for the moment. The wax could wait, simmering over the flames. The provisioner, his gaunt face lined with wrinkles under his fringe of grey hair, drew his spare frame close and smiled thinly.

"It seems that your friend over there"—he tilted his head towards John—"did not take your jest amiss. Indeed, he spoke to me of your earnest desire to try your hand at illustration."

"Ay, Brother, I'd love that."

The severe features of the amarius crinkled into an encouraging smile.

"I will speak with the chandler this afternoon. If he agrees to relinquish you, I will give you a week's trial to gauge your suitability."

Back to my boiler, the chandler drew me aside to remark on his satisfaction with my work, but give him his due, he grinned and quoted the Gospel of Matthew, "Jesus says: *Neither do men light a candle, and put it under a bushel, but on a candlestick; and it giveth light unto all that are in the house. Let your light so shine before men, that they may see your good works, and glorify your Father which is in heaven.*"

I matched his grin and said, "I'll wager all your quotes from the Bible mention candles!"

He laughed, clapped me on the back and added, "If you have a talent, you should use it to the glory of God, Asher. I can soon find a pair of willing hands to take your place. I hope the next one is as hard-working as you."

So, we parted amicably, with me entering the scriptorium

11

to John's friendly smile and a nod of encouragement. The provisioner, Brother Adelbrand, for that was his name, allocated a desk to me, well-lit under a window, and gave me the benefit of his advice that lasted all morning. After lunch, he set me some exercises, copying scrolls and initials. It was enjoyable, but not creative. Satisfied, he placed a hand lightly on my shoulder and said, "Very good, Asher. Now I want you to lay out a full page illustrating the parable of the Sower."

With hindsight, this was far too difficult a task to set a beginner to, but the provisioner must have seen something promising in my work. The centrepiece, the Sower himself, scattering seed, his head surrounded by a whirl of crows was coming along well until Brother Ganthar bumped into my elbow. Although he apologised profusely, I know that it was a deliberate act of sabotage. The jolt sent my quill scratching across the page but my wits came to my rescue. Converting the line into the ridge of a furrow, the illustration was not compromised.

Before Vespers, Ganthar returned to the scene of his misdemeanour,

"I hope I did not ruin your..." his voice trailed away as he gaped at my lovely interpretation of the parable. The borders with their miniatures and scrolls were not yet completed but the effect was captivating. I dislike false modesty as much as boastfulness—I speak plainly.

"Not at all, Brother Ganthar, your clumsiness helped me improve the design."

His only reply was "Harumph!" and he walked away without a word of praise. That came instead when my day's work was over in time for the evening service. The provisioner squeezed my arm and said, "Your week's trial is over in only one day. Well done, Brother Asher! It is hard to believe that you have never illustrated before. You have a God-given talent. Isn't that so, Brother John? I think that Brother Asher will help you with your evangeliary; since the parable of the Sower is often read during the liturgy, you can incorporate this wonderful illustration. Now, we must hurry to Vespers."

On our way to the church, John said, "I'm delighted we can work together. You'll do the illustrations and I will take care of the writing. We'll talk in more detail after the service."

"Good. There's something else I need to ask you later." I had Brother Ganthar on my mind.

After Vespers, we sat on a low wall enjoying the warm evening sun where I told him about the episode with the pinch-faced monk.

"You are right about him. I had occasion to complain to Brother Adelbrand after my best quill went missing. I accused no one, merely pointing out its disappearance, but the amarius told me to be wary of Brother Ganthar. He told me that the poor fellow had come to the monastery a wretched boy, as a refuge from violent, uncaring parents. The provisioner says he is damaged. He hinted that Ganthar might be a little unhinged. Undoubtedly, he has a spiteful side to his nature and often shows his jealousy, especially of friends—since he has none of his own."

"We'll have to be careful, then," I said, nudging John. It was meant to be a light-hearted comment, but John grew silent, frowned and hummed, nodding with pursed lips.

Feeling that I should not leave the conversation dangling, I said, "I've noticed that he's unpopular and the others shun him. Outside of the scriptorium, he latches onto anyone he can find and begins tedious speeches on any subject that comes to his mind. He always centres the discussion on himself: *I* is his most frequent word, interspersed with *let me finish* or *you know what I think?* He wants to be the centre of attention."

"Don't you feel sorry for him?" John asked, giving me a sidelong glance.

"Well, I suppose with such a troubled childhood, it's understandable. But if he nudges my arm again, I won't refrain from confronting him."

"Since we are going to work together on the evangeliary, you can take the seat next to the wall and I'll sit by the aisle. In that way, he won't be able to brush against you. It's a shame; he has excellent penmanship, you know."

"His eyes are too close set for my liking."

"My *nose* is too big for your liking!"

I was distracted talking about the spiteful monk, so he caught me unawares. I gazed at his face and said, "No, it isn't. It's normal: just right for your face."

"Ha! I knew it—you have a cruel sense of humour, Asher. So, you see, nobody is perfect."

He was referring to my caricature, of course, but he had made his point. I would have to cut Brother Ganthar some slack. I was not oblivious to the illustrator's unsettling constant glances across the room as John and I discussed our work. My friend was writing the Beatitudes from Jesus's Sermon on the Mount in the minuscule script introduced by Charlemagne's reforms. We agreed that these lines were not suited to illustration.

"Don't worry. Next, I'm going to write the account in the Gospel of John, the one where Mary is weeping at Jesus's empty tomb and sees the two angels. Surely, that lends itself to your colours."

An unsolicited voice intervened.

"I know how I would do that: I'd have her wet-eyed turning to address the gardener."

Ganthar had sidled over to eavesdrop on our conversation. I

repeated his words in my head and counted: sixteen words and three of them had been 'I'.

"Thank you for your advice, Brother Ganthar," I forced myself to say. "But, you know, everybody has to work in his own way."

"Ay, well, with you being new here and all, I thought you might need a hand. Tell you what, I'll sketch you an outline of what you should do."

I bit my tongue and did not reply, but watched him walk away.

"Ignore him. Do it your own way," John whispered, reflecting my thoughts.

There was no stopping him, for within the hour Ganthar was back, flourishing vellum under my nose. I had to admit, he had a fine hand and had produced a worthy sketch in black ink.

"There, that's the way it should be done! Feel free to come to me if you experience difficulties. I'll leave it with you. I'll come over now and again to keep an eye on your progress."

"That won't be necessary," I said through clenched teeth. The entrance to the tomb was skilfully drawn and, feeling it would be a shame to waste it I copied it onto my parchment. The way he had depicted the angels did not suit me, so I inked in figures that pleased me more, changing their positions according to the Gospel account, not Ganthar's. Soon, I had completed my outline to my satisfaction. But here he came again, squinting and craning over John's head to catch a glimpse of my design.

"No, no, no! That will never do! I'll have to show you, that's all there is for it." He spun his skinny frame and hurried to his desk, staring from there across at me with a scowl before rearranging parchment on his workspace and bowing his head intently over his work. He was still busy when the bells called us to the service that marked the end of the day's chores. As usual, I strolled to the church with John, occasionally casting an anxious glance behind. There was no sign of Ganthar following us from the scriptorium. I assumed he was putting a finishing touch to whatever he was working on. It was unthinkable to be late for the compulsory Vespers.

Not until the next day did I discover what the sly fellow had been up to. When I sat at my desk, where my half-finished illustration should have been, lay a full-colour version of the Lord's tomb. The page was complete with exquisite borders. In truth, it was a splendid effort. Brother Ganthar was staring at us from his place across the room with a gargoyle grin on his narrow face. He must have worked until late to finish the illustration.

"Ah, well, you'd better have this, John," I said, with a sigh.

My friend took it, glanced briefly at the small masterpiece, stood and took two steps toward Ganthar, slowly and deliberately ripped the page in half.

"It's no use to me." He glared at the shocked monk. "The illustrations in my evangeliary must all be in the same style, by the same hand, and that will be Asher's." He crumpled the remnants in his large fist and tossed the ball of parchment at the distraught illustrator.

"You've made an enemy there, John," I whispered.

"I don't care. He makes my skin crawl."

Searching among my belongings, to my annoyance, I failed to find my previous day's work. Before I could vent my wrath on the discomfited monk, he came over clutching a piece of vellum.

"This is yours," he said, his head down, eyes downcast and voice humble. I was feeling sorry for him when he added, "At least you know how it should be done. I'd start again if I were you."

I snatched the sheet from him and snarled, "Thank you. As I said, everybody must work in his way."

As my illustration progressed, with John in silent concentration, I wrestled with my thoughts, which centred on the skinny fellow across the room. Uneasily, I dwelt on his spiteful nature and worried that, in some way, he would gain revenge for John's actions.

THREE

FULDA, HESSE, 830 – 842 AD

Our early years in Fulda not only consolidated our firm friendship but John and I also served a thorough preparation for our later lives. In this, I cannot praise enough our amarius, Brother Adelbrand, who was a man of most acute intelligence, immensely learned in all fields of literary endeavour, and extremely ingenious in the art of illustration. I am displeased that this modest man never attained the reputation he deserved.

The ordered routine of monastic life provided little scope for excitement, but occasionally minor episodes took on disproportionate importance, like the constant irritation caused by the petty thieving of the rogue Ganthar. Small items regularly disappeared to the annoyance of the owners. Everybody knew or suspected the culprit but nothing happened to him until John, tired of his purloining, lay in wait for him in the scriptorium. Alerted by the envious glances of the weaselly monk directed at his sharp, bone-handled penknife, my friend left it lying in plain sight on his work surface before heading to Vespers. Slipping out unnoticed, before the Benediction of the

Blessed Sacrament, he hurried to the scriptorium and hid on the dais behind the provisioner's desk.

As he expected, the door opened silently to reveal Ganthar's head peering warily within to ensure the place was deserted. The thief slipped inside, with short furtive steps reached John's workplace, then, snatching up the penknife, he held it before his gloating face and pocketed it. When he turned to sneak out, a large hand grasped his bony shoulder, making him squeal and wriggle.

However, there was no escaping the iron grasp.

"At last, I've caught you in the act! Now, I'm giving you two choices: either you take me to your stash and surrender it or I'm going to beat you until I break your every rib. Do not put me to the test, *Brother* Ganthar!" He sneered the formal title to stress the flagrant breach of fraternity carried out by the thief.

"All right, all right! Don't hurt me. Take your knife, but I swear I took nothing else!"

"Maybe not tonight, rascal, but what about Brother Asher's best quill? Do you want me to take you before the whole monastery and have them list their missing belongings, or shall we keep this between us?"

"Ah, I see!" A hideous grin distorted the pinched features. "You want to split my loot! You're as crafty as I am! Ow!"

John's open hand dealt a stinging slap across the felon's ear and sent him staggering into a desk, before the taller man's hand grasped the front of his tunic and hauled him within inches of his angry face. Eyeball to eyeball, John glared.

"Do not dare associate me with your vile ways, scum! Not unless you want me to start on your scrawny ribs!"

"Nay, Brother, mercy! I meant no harm. I'll take you to my horde. I swear I will!"

Not releasing his grip on the skinny shoulder, John followed the pilferer into the monastery stables. The disgraced monk led him to the back wall and pointed to one of the stones. On inspection, the mortar had been dug away and the stone could be eased out.

"You're used to removing it," John growled. "Get on with it."

Inside the wall cavity, some rubble had been dug out to create a space filled by a wooden box. On closer scrutiny, it was a drawer—one that had disappeared from the scriptorium to the annoyance of the provisioner, who had been forced to call upon a woodworker to make him a replacement. The delinquent laid the drawer on the straw-covered stone floor and, bending over, John picked out a key.

"What does this open?" He glared at the trembling monk.

"I don't remember."

A fist hammered into the cur's side and he screamed.

"How's your memory now?"

Tears swilled down Ganthar's cheeks as he bent and rubbed his ribs.

"I'll tell you everything! Don't hit me again, please! It opens the pantry door."

"Well, I'm sure the Cellarer will be pleased to have it back."

"Oh, no. You won't tell him I took it, will you?"

"Nay, Brother, *you* will!" John left the box on the stable floor, grasping the thief with one hand and the key with the other. He marched Ganthar to the refectory.

To cut a long story short, the outraged Cellarer, understanding, at last, why his provisions occasionally did not tally with his inventory, insisted on taking the crooked monk to Abbot Rabanus Maurus, who, on ascertaining all the facts, expelled the thief from the monastery without compunction.

For all his vengeful curses and threats, we did not expect to see Ganthar again. How sadly mistaken we were! The passing of six years without setting eyes on the shifty-eyed individual lulled us into forgetting about him. Meanwhile, our abbot, Rabanus Maurus, summoned us into his quarters, which we thought strange. Why the two of us should be convoked together had us baffled.

The superior revelled in our perplexity.

"Brothers, you will be wondering why I asked you both to meet with me. I suggest you consider what skills you share. Brother John, you have the neatest hand in the monastery. Rarely, or never, do you make a mistake. And you, Brother Asher, are the finest illustrator among your peers. That is why you are standing here."

"May I speak, Father?" John asked.

"Please do."

John looked from my curious face to that of the grey-haired monk.

"We are grateful for your kind words, Father Abbot, but what is it you require of us?"

"Patience is a virtue, Brother John. It is one you should cultivate more assiduously. I was just coming to my explanation. Have either of you seen a copy of the *De Laudibus Sanctae Crucis?*"

The moment had come for me to speak.

"Indeed, Father Abbot. We had the good fortune to study it when one arrived here lately, illuminated by brothers of the Tours Scriptorium. It is a marvel!"

"Just so! But not as great a wonder as what we shall produce. Our version is destined for the Emperor himself. Brother John, I will dictate and you will write. As for you, Brother Asher, each of your illustrations will contain the repetitive sign of the Cross or a crucifix. Your first task will be to capture my likeness in a dedicatory image, with me presenting the gift to Pope Gregory. I also require you to represent

21

Emperor Louis as *miles christianus*. Do you think you can manage that?"

"Of course, Father."

"Excellent. You will have free rein for the other images in the book and will work as usual in the scriptorium, whereas you, Brother John, will bring your quill and ink to this desk." He indicated a chair and escritoire with a sweep of his hand.

As we walked away, John complained.

"My poor eyes! Give me the grace, Lord, to accept what I cannot change."

"Why, what's the matter, my friend? Are you not delighted to be working alone with the abbot? He is renowned for his learning."

"I know, but did you not see how badly lit is his desk? Not like the scriptorium where we are blessed with our large window."

I was sure to miss my workbench companion, but thanked the Lord that I had studied the miniatures from Tours so that I would produce work in a similar style. Fourteen months later, the abbot declared his satisfaction at the completed volume.

"I particularly like your rendition of the *miles christianus*, Brother Asher. It is sure to please the Emperor. See, Brother John, how your friend has the subject holding a cross-topped staff in his right hand and a shield emblazoned with a cross in his left hand." Actually, I was rather pleased with the breast-plate over the chiton down to the knees, not to mention the minute letters on the halo declaring *You Christ crown Louis*, but the abbot did not refer to them.

To this day, I remain well satisfied with my work on the *De Laudibus Sanctae Crucis*, but was forced to reevaluate my skills when we travelled to Reims to present the gift to Emperor Louis the Pious. The Reims scriptorium was second only to Tours. John and I feasted our eyes on the production of the scribes and each made treasure of the new techniques, which served to bathe us in humility.

On our return to Fulda, we conferred and agreed that the time had come for us to leave for pastures new. We had seen enough at Reims to realise that only in such a scriptorium would we fulfil our potential. John had a thirst for learning: seeing the volumes available for reading there fired his enthusiasm. Underlying his ambition was his high-achieving family. He had not known his father, the count, who died a year after his birth, whose widow was now universally acclaimed as a saint for her life devoted to the poor. One brother had reached the station of an abbot, while his sister, Addila, was abbess of Herzfeld.

"Look at me," John grumbled to me on one occasion when talking about his kinsfolk, "I am nought but an unworthy scribbler."

The conviction grew that we had to leave the idyllic life at Fulda since we had both passed our thirtieth winter. The notion *now or never* became impelling. However, it was not exact. The most unlikely events ensured that.

Rebellion burst forth in Saxony involving the two classes of freemen below the nobility but above the unfree. Following the conversion to Christianity enforced by the Franks, these men had lost their rights and were little better than peasants. They despised the *Lex Saxonum* of Charlemagne and sought to live again according to tribal custom. Many were deeply anti-Christian and some flirted with a return to paganism. I do not believe they were pagans but rather people who longed for justice, more of a guild than a revolutionary movement.

Still, they took advantage of the civil wars between Louis and his sons. When Lothar canvassed support from the Stellinga, as they were called, he promised them they could keep the law which their ancestors kept. It was enough for them to unite with him and his leading men.

You may ask how this affected our monastery. It is here that we meet Ganthar again. He had thrown in his lot with the Stellinga and as a former monk at Fulda, his comrades chose him as an envoy to persuade the abbot to renounce ties with the local nobility. Abbot Rabanus Maurus had no such intentions, because many nobles had donated land to the monastery in exchange for prayers for their souls.

Our erstwhile pilferer-turned-politician spoke to John and me, knowing that we once wielded arms. This was true and although we had been rebels in our youth, our lives, values and ambitions had changed.

"Come, fight with us, Brothers. Help us take back our lost rights. We can no longer serve the corrupt, grasping rich men." His narrow face contorted, making his features more repulsive. "If you are not with us, you are *against* us, and Fulda will burn."

John lurched forward and, not for the first time, delivered a stinging slap to the rascal's ear.

"Get out of my sight!" bellowed my friend.

Backing away, ready to run, his spittle flying, Ganthar threatened, "I'll see that you are the first to feel cold steel, *Brother* John."

We watched him run away to John's muttered, "Good riddance!"

I turned to face my friend. "Do you think these rebels will attack Fulda?"

"The abbot is aligned with the nobility. We may yet have to take up arms, but it is not our decision. Patience is a virtue, Brother," he quoted the abbot.

I looked into his face with its firm, determined chin and deep-set, honest eyes, and felt reassured.

The weeks passed, news filtering through because, though the monastery was in Hesse, it held lands in Saxony where the unrest was centred. At last, the abbot called a meeting in our chapter house.

"Brothers, a grave threat hangs over our peaceful existence. The rebels have entered our region; thus, the Count is calling on all able-bodied men to take up arms in defence of his territory. Our monastery lies amid his lands. Therefore, I have promised to offer dispensation to any of you brothers who wish to, how shall I put this?" He coughed to cover his unease. "To fight to preserve our tranquillity and service to the Lord."

"Ay, I'll fight," growled John and heads turned to gape at him.

The abbot's face showed satisfaction when several more voices declared in favour of fighting.

I added mine to this small chorus, less out of conviction than a determination not to be separated from my best friend.

"All brothers who wish to depart to fight for a just cause will now gather in the courtyard. The rest into the church, at once." Thus declared the abbot, and we filed out in different directions. Our Superior bade us kneel, whereupon he blessed us and repeated his conviction that our small band would fight in a just cause. Our surprise was enormous when he led us to a storeroom that not one brother had ever entered. He sorted through keys on a large ring he took out from his pocket, grunted in satisfaction, and forced the unyielding lock to turn.

"Arm yourselves, and may God be with you!"

That was how we discovered that there was an arms cache in Fulda. We found swords, axes, spears, and helms. I latched onto one of the few pieces of body armour before anyone else grabbed it, a tough leather breastplate. Ensuring I was well-equipped for battle, I asked John, "Why do you think there was an arms deposit in the monastery?"

"I should think these weapons date from the dark days when Saxon pagans descended upon the monks, who had to defend these walls.

"Those days are back," I said bitterly.

"They are not. These Stellinga are not pagans. They wish to rise socially—like Ganthar, they would take what is not theirs."

"Yet, he spoke of lost rights," I wondered uneasily.

"Cheap words! The Empire has brought stability and wealth. Just look to our eastern borders and how the Count has quelled the onslaughts of the Abodrites and Sorbs against our people. Peace and prosperity can only be bought in blood, I fear."

John was a strong-minded fellow and always saw things clearly, so I set aside my doubts. We marched out of the monastery to join with the nobles and other churchmen to fight the insurgents.

After years of wielding quills, I wondered how my body would fare in combat. I didn't have long to wait, because the Bishop of Mainz at the head of his force with the Stellinga were marching south towards us.

FOUR

The weaving of fate reminds me of the moods of the ocean: one day flat and calm, the next erupting into towering waves capable of sweeping or submerging everything in its relentless path. My weary memory has no difficulty recalling the events of the fateful event that engulfed us sixty-three summers past.

When our small band of warrior-monks joined the count's forces, we thought we were marching to clash with the oncoming rebels. Instead, our vanguard surprised us by veering away towards the south-west. Unsuspectingly, we had committed ourselves to a forced march of over two hundred leagues that dragged on for five weeks. Word filtered down the ranks from our leaders that we were to join forces to combat a threat to the Empire.

"We have left the way open for an attack on Fulda," John said one evening, gazing with forlorn expression at the faces glowing red around the flickering campfire.

"Ay, we should have stood our ground and put an end to them before they reached the monastery walls," I contributed, little knowing that the foe, summoned like us, was on a parallel march.

Under the same misapprehension, Brother Theobald, his anguished voice belying his mighty stature, expressed the thought that troubled us all,

"Who can say what fate has befallen our brethren within the walls of Fulda?"

John's calm tone reassured us and eased our worries. "Abbot Rabanus Maurus is a wily old fox; he will have found the means of saving our brothers and the monastery."

A late evening discussion followed on what might or might not have transpired there. Only the indignant orders of our officers put an end to the futile speculation.

"Get you to your beds! I'll have no slacking on the morrow!" bellowed a seasoned veteran of many campaigns, whom we nicknamed *Ossie the Ogre* because his name was Oslac, whose bewhiskered face and half-mad eyes induced terror in anyone who occasioned his wrath. Later, we came to admire the courage and ferocity of this warrior when he begot the same dread in our foes in combat.

Our long march was uneventful except for a natural foreboding when we penetrated deeply into the great forest of the Ardennes. It must be human nature to recount tales designed to play on man's most deep-seated fears. Perversely, that is what happened around the campfire in the depths of the woodland. The unsettling howls in the distance added to the impenetrable blackness amid the trees that concealed bears, boars, and restless wolves.

"It's not wild beasts that worry me," said a timorous youth, his callow visage coloured by the dancing flames, "it's the wraiths, trolls and elves," he pointed a shaking finger into the darkness, "that live in caves and hollow trees."

This pronouncement was followed by a long silence,

broken at last by the calm, sensible voice of John. In a flat tone, he delivered as he looked from one to the other, "Are we no better than the pagans of yesteryear? Do not heed this superstitious nonsense. Have you no shame, boy?" He gave the youth a withering stare. "The wild beasts fear our fires and our numbers and have slunk far away. As for your monsters, they do not exist. Put your faith in the Lord, who will provide you with a shield against demons."

"Sorry," murmured the young man, accepting the drinking horn passed from man to man.

The silence of reflection as each man weighed John's words was broken when he spoke again.

"In the end, it comes down to *men*. It is they we must contend with; they are the reason why we find ourselves here today. The only monster hereabouts is Ossie." He grinned.

We all laughed, looking nervously around to make sure that the bane of our lives was not in the vicinity. He was not. The officers were all gathered in the pavilion of our leader Louis, known as *the German*, who was the grandson of Charlemagne and third son of Louis the Pious. In the aftermath of the cataclysm we were about to face, he would become the king of East Frankia. This meeting, had we understood its importance, signalled the convergence of the opposing armies. The enemy was still several days march distant. We did not know the lie of the land, but to our relief, we left the forest the next day. At the back of our minds, we had crossed it with the constant anxiety that our scouts might miss an ambush; that our fears were ridiculous became apparent later when we faced the mighty unconcealable host of our foes.

Unknown to us as we approached Auxerre, we were about to fight in the greatest battle of the age. Much has been discussed and written about the Battle of Fontenoy, but on that June day, my companions and I were unsure of why we were fighting. Most certainly, it was not a battle against the Stellinga as we thought when we enrolled. Rather, we were caught up in a war of greed and power. The sons and nephews of Louis the Pious contended territorial inheritances—in other words, a squabble over the division of Charlemagne's great Empire. Call what happened that day a squabble! Nay, it was more a clash of the Titans. Never had so many gathered to fight on behalf of so few. It is not within my failing powers to describe adequately what I saw that day. Luckily, one of our enemies, the poet, Angilbert, versified this epic battle in which he fought on the losing side but survived to leave his splendid poem.

I will transcribe here only the fourth of the seven verses to give an idea of the horror of that day. I will set down the whole in an Appendix at the end of my tale. His powerful image captures in a few lines what my memory balks at reliving:

On the side alike of Louis, on the side of Charles alike,
Lies the field in white enshrouded, in the vestments of
the dead,
As it lies when birds in autumn settle white off the
shore.

How to describe a battle on so large a scale, and to remember it without exaggeration or false glorification? Ay, the clash resulted in our victory, changing the course of nations and individual lives. But all I can do is write about the smaller world that heaved and swirled around me as the slaughter played out as far as my horrified eye could see.

Close to our small group, John and Oslac fought as men possessed. Their axes accounted for the enemy corpses piled up before us. I held my own against the onslaught and slew five warriors in the enemy front line. At one point, I slipped on the blood underfoot, causing me to finish on one knee. It was my moment of greatest peril. I raised my shield above my head just in time, as a mighty axe blow juddered through my arm, rocking my whole body. From my low position, under my shield, I could see only the legs of my assailant. Rapid as a striking viper, I sliced my sword behind his knee, severing the sinews and sending him screaming to the ground where the man next to me finished him with his axe.

After that narrow escape, the fighting continued until twilight, confused, noisy and muscle-searing. Weariness throughout my body and in a different way, in my head, meant that I understood little of what happened around me. I functioned only on instinct and reactions. At a certain point near the day's end, hoarse cheers broke from the throats of my comrades, which as I drove my sword under the shield of an adversary, told me that the day was ours. Confirmation came when John stepped over bodies to join and embrace me. At that moment, it was a welcome gesture, but at any other time, his gore-soaked armour would have been repugnant to me. Instead, we hopped and swayed, dizzy with fatigue, cheering along with our comrades as the realisation dawned that we were alive and victorious among the dead whose gruesome corpses lay strewn as far as the eye could see.

As old age approached, John and I read various accounts of what happened that day. Setting aside the many unreliable tales that men are wont to recount, I will attempt the briefest of summaries. The inescapable fact is that on both sides, the dead totalled 40,000—a slaughter hitherto unmatched to my knowledge. The events, so confused on the day, can now be briefly related as follows: our leader, Charles established our camp at Thury, on the hill of Roichat. Lothair and Pepin initiated battle and took the upper hand until the arrival of Guerin and the men of Provence. While Pepin and his force continued to push back Charles's men, led by Louis the German, we slowly repulsed Lothair. Finally, when victory seemed sure for Charles, Bernard of Septimania entered the conflict on our side, so the day ended in a rout.

Hostilities continued for another two years into 843, but the Treaty of Verdun ended the war and reshaped Europe forever. My life and that of John also changed after the battle.

"Brother Asher, fate has brought us far from Fulda. I have decided I will not return."

We discovered by asking our comrades that our position near Fontenoy was distant from the two places that interested us most. As John said, "We should go either to Tours or Reims to study and improve our skills. I have no desire to continue wielding arms."

By careful questioning and checking, we discovered that Tours lay 57 leagues to the west, whereas we would reach Reims, distant 42 leagues, with a day's less marching. Knowing already what Reims had to offer and it also being a royal burgh, it seemed the correct choice to both of us and one we would not regret.

Although we travelled alone, we arrived unmolested. Likely our armour and weapons discouraged the ill-intentioned. The ancient abbey in Reims, dedicated to Saint Remy and founded on his relics, was the richest in Frankia. The abbey boasted 700 domains and, as we knew, vaunted an important book collection and much book production, thus making it a centre for the dissemination of ancient culture throughout the West. The latter was what drove John to march to Reims. Once established in the abbey, he spent whatever free time he had devouring the contents of Greek texts until he became a paragon of culture. But I get ahead of my tale.

When we arrived in the monastery, our tonsures testimony of our vows, we were honoured as victors over the rebels and allowed to speak with the amarius in the renowned scriptorium.

"Brothers, if your account is true, we will make good use of you in our midst. However, you will understand my qualms. As with any newcomer, I must put your abilities to the test as our standards are amongst the highest in Frankia."

We knew this to be so and readily acceded to his request.

"Excellent!" His rotund, benign countenance turned a fulsome smile on John. "Then you, Brother, will write from memory in your best hand Psalm 20." He turned to me, saying, "And you, Brother"—he rubbed his hands together in a gesture of enthusiasm—"will illustrate the psalm."

John's task was decidedly easier, because as we know, Psalm 20 has only nine lines. The amarius accommodated us at a wide desk and provided the vellum and inks we required.

"Remember, I expect your very best work," he admonished.

John had already written the first line:

May the LORD answer you when you are in distress; may the name of the God of Jacob protect you.

How to capture the psalm visually? Maybe the experience of the last few weeks had addled my brain. I considered the easiest option of designing an intricate large first initial, in this case, the M; but soon dismissed this as too trite. Reciting the psalm in my head, inspiration came at line three:

May he remember all your sacrifices and accept your burnt offerings.

Determined, I drew a man wearing a swirling purple robe, standing in supplication before an altar, arms raised overhead with a bowl cupped in both hands. Smoke swirled around him rising from the hidden surface of the sacred table. As a frame, I created a portico with a triangular pediment supported by fluted columns: the effect was harmonious and appealing, as confirmed by the provisioner, who clapped his chubby hands in appreciation and welcomed us into the scriptorium. Again he clapped his hands, but this time loudly to attract the attention of the scribes,

"Brothers, I bid you to welcome among us our newest and talented *soci*." Occasionally, he sprinkled Latin words into his everyday speech. "I feel sure you will make them feel at home." Those words were prescient, because when we withdrew to the frater for lunch, we were the centre of much kindly attention. The brothers explained that the archbishop of Reims was also the abbot.

One talkative scribe, a fellow with striking corn-coloured hair and somewhat thick lips, set down his spoon to reveal, "The present incumbent, Ebbo, has had a chequered history since he was obliged to resign six years ago. Did you know he supported the elder sons of Emperor Louis in their rebellion?" He paused and raised a quizzical eyebrow, continuing with gusto when we both shook our heads, "When Lothair had to flee to Italy, Ebbo was too ill with gout to follow and took shelter with a Parisian hermit, would you believe? Louis's men found and imprisoned him in your old Abbey of Fulda."

"That must have been who the secret prisoner was. We never did find out," I whispered to John, who nodded.

"Now we know," he murmured in my ear. We returned to listening to the informative monk.

"So, the abbey did without an abbot until he was restored by our gracious emperor in June last year. Abbot Ebbo is a good and learned man, but too involved in worldly matters— although, that is only my opinion for what it's worth," he ended edgily.

"Thank you, Brother, for your interesting information." John scratched an ear with his forefinger and looked earnestly at his colleague. "You said the abbot is learned. What makes you say that?"

The talkative young monk frowned and thought for a while. Another companion cut in; he had a large mole above his upper lip that distracted me as he spoke. "It is true, Abbot Ebbo can speak many languages and is a great collector of texts, especially ancient manuscripts. He uses his position of archbishop to bring new volumes within these walls whenever he travels."

"That's right," joined in the first monk, "he has a penchant for Greek texts. The abbot is most impatient that none among us scribes speaks that language."

"I do," John murmured, but they heard him.

"You should tell that to the provisioner, Brother. He'll be delighted. It's a pity our Superior is away at the moment. He is at the imperial court in Aachen. These are troubled times as *you two* know only too well! It is a journey of sixty leagues from here, so we don't know when he'll be back."

John showed particular interest in the discussion and asked many questions about the Greek texts. The upshot was that the corn-haired monk volunteered to intervene with the provisioner. This promise he maintained, so that instead of setting us further tasks the amarius led us into a library attached to the scriptorium where John was destined to spend innumerable hours of study. We soon discovered that chubby Provisioner Richomer was an opportunist.

"Ha! Here is a Greek text. It's a *liber comitis*. Can you translate it, Brother John?"

My friend took the slim, crimson-bound leather volume eagerly. Opening it carefully, he read two lines. "Which means ..." How can I report it? To my shame, at my advanced age I still cannot read Greek, but suffice to say, he translated the Greek into Latin effortlessly, provoking the chubby hands to applaud enthusiastically again.

"Well then, Brother John, you are most proficient! What do you say to transcribing this lectionary into Latin, so that we shall surprise Abbot Ebbo with a gift upon his return? You, Brother Asher, will further beautify John's work."

That is what we did, finishing the book intended to be read at divine service a matter of two weeks before the abbot's return. This was fortuitous timing. It gave the brothers time to prepare the ornate leather cover on its wooden boards: not a job one can complete overnight. Brother Richomer was ecstatic with the completed volume, disappearing into the library to fetch the Greek version. Setting one beside the other on his desk, he beamed,

"There's no comparison. See how shabby the original volume appears next to our *liber comitis!*"

"That's unfair!" John whispered in my ear, "The Greek text is very ancient and yet so well expressed."

Enclosed in our scriptural sanctuary, we had no idea that Abbot Ebbo had returned until the beatific countenance of our amarius grinned at us.

"Father Abbot is delighted with your work, Brothers. He compared the two texts and found yours, in his words, '*quite splendid*'! He wishes to see you both in his quarters, immediately."

The abbot's room, as befitting an archbishop, was resplendent with gilded imagery and exquisitely carved furniture. One icon of the Virgin took my breath away. On seeing my reaction, Abbot Ebbo said with an air of satisfaction, "You must be the illustrator, Brother Asher. I see that you have an eye for beauty. This icon hails from Constantinople." He turned to John and said something I did not understand. My friend replied equally unintelligibly; I guessed correctly that they were conversing in ancient Greek.

Returning to our language, the abbot said, "I gather you are from Fulda. I imagine you have better memories of that place than I."

We exchanged glances. I spoke as politely as I knew how, "Father, we learnt from the brothers that you were there in unfortunate circumstances, unknown to us, before we left the monastery."

"*Errare humanum est, ignoscere divinum,*" he quoted. "However, our gracious Emperor divinely forgave my error and here I am. Fulda must have much to recommend it since it produced two such fine scribes."

"Thank you, Father Abbot." John inclined his head respectfully.

"This will be your role from now on. I will provide the Greek texts and you, Brother John, will convert them into Latin. I think we can rely on Brother Asher to illuminate the text, don't you?"

"Without doubt, Father."

That became our continuous task, working on psalters, lectionaries, evangeliaries and even on a sacramentary for the archbishop's personal use. We did this until the benevolent superior passed away in 851. It proved to be wonderful preparation for the event that would definitively change our lives.

FIVE

The archbishopric of Reims passed to a greater man than Ebbo in 845 with the consecration of Hincmar. Although, on that day in early May, neither of us had an inkling of how his mandate would affect us. I can, with hindsight, reveal that it was providential. A man of learning and culture, he soon discovered evidence of our activities under his predecessor and, captivated by our skills, sent us away.

An obsession or passion for ancient texts that eclipsed Ebbo's led him to establish an important scriptorium in a place six leagues farther south, situated in a forest and on a hill. Less than another league in the same direction flowed the River Marne. That was a worry, but more about that anon. Hincmar desired for this scriptorium to be the most renowned in the West.

"Look what I have laid hands on, Brothers," he said with barely concealed gloating. We set down our pens then moved closer to peer at a volume reduced to a very poor condition. "This text survived Theophilus and the fire in Alexandria. I am sure it was old even then. I would calculate its age at seven hundred years."

John reached for it, but the archbishop stepped away, shaking his head.

"Nay, it is very delicate and must be placed with absolute care on a flat surface. Are you aware of what this text contains?"

Our turn had come to shake our heads. Without inspecting it, how were we supposed to know? The question was rhetorical, because he went on to explain in that strange nasal voice of his, so contrasting with his refined speech and distinguished appearance.

"My dear scribes, this is the production of an unknown author. It goes by the title of *Physiologus*, a didactic Christian text explaining the symbolic nature of beasts."

"How very interesting," John intervened. "I assume the writing is in Greek."

"Oh, indeed, this volume is already translated into Latin. That was first achieved over four hundred years ago. But my dear scribes, having satisfied myself that your translating abilities are of the highest order, as are your skills at depiction, I bethought it an exceedingly splendid notion to have you render it with miniatures unframed and set in the text block." The archbishop loved to vaunt his education in overblown language. "What say you, good fellows?"

"Ay, Father," John replied, ironically matching the archbishop's high-flown language. "It will be an immense privilege to produce a modern version of that olden classical script."

The archbishop glowed and expressed his pleasure immediately by placing the manuscript with extreme delicacy on a flat, wooden desk. "Come, feast your eyes on the lion"—he translated the ancient Greek effortlessly—"whose cubs are born dead and receive life when the old lion breathes upon them."

He looked up triumphantly. "You, of course, understand the allegory underlying the tale?"

I had no idea what he was talking about, but as ever, John's sharp intelligence saved me from embarrassment. "The lion represents Christ while the cubs are the symbol for Mankind. It is a message of salvation."

"I knew it! I was sure I could entrust this task to your capable hands. You will find similar elucidations with many creatures throughout the work. Such as the unicorn which only permits itself to be captured in the lap of a pure virgin. You will understand it as a type of the Incarnation. But I must not allow my enthusiasm to spoil your discovery of the enchanting contents, Brothers," he purred. Then the astonishing revelation that we should travel to Hautvillers, carrying the manuscript in a specially constructed container, he reserved for last.

He failed to mention that the transfer would be permanent.

It was this uprooting that saved us from the terrible fate of Reims Abbey. When we were both children growing up in Saxony, we had never heard of the Vikings. Yet, in our years of innocent playfulness, the Norsemen had already attacked the western coast of Frankia. At the time of our arrival in Hautvillers, the Emperor Charles the Bald was paying tribute to keep the sea-wolves from ravaging his lands. In our seclusion within the walls of Reims Abbey, we knew nothing of this. Nor did we learn of the Emperor's bold decision to face the raiders and vanquish them in open combat. At that point we resided in our new monastery in the depths of a forest isolated from the world. Not that the abbey was completely unknown to the outside world—not many years before our arrival, in 841, a priest from Reims stole the relic of the body of Saint Helena from Rome and the reliquary was transferred to our abbey. The relics attracted pilgrims, so the revenues allowed the abbey to purchase lands and vineyards in the vicinity. By the time we had arrived, there must have been 40 hectares of ordered vines. Thus, John and I were not short of a beaker of wine during our permanence.

However, I will set aside mention of the Vikings for the moment because I must explain the nature of our work on the *Physiologus* that became our daily occupation for several years. This volume alone established our reputation and brought us recognition from far afield. In turn, it would lead us overseas, but more of that further into my tale.

Once settled into our new abbey and its scriptorium under the benevolent eye of the provisioner, we started upon our masterpiece. The short-sighted amarius, with his white hair, round face, and small nose, reminded me of a barn owl. The poor man seemed in awe of the recommendations sent by the archbishop, which preceded our arrival, but it meant that whatever we desired was, for him, never too much trouble.

That first morning, John unpacked the manuscript with extreme care, laying it on a specially requisitioned table beside our desk. Bending over it, he gently turned the first page, sighed, fixed me with an unsettling stare accompanied with a prolonged silence before stating, "Asher, remember that every creature of the world is like a book and a picture to us, and a mirror."

I do not know whether he was quoting some higher authority, for his tone was suitably grave. Then he added, "Never lose sight of that notion during our reproduction of this text, Brother." His hand stroked the page as a lover might caress his betrothed. "Now, my friend, I must explain the structure of the volume we have agreed to produce so that, with an overview, you will know how best to lay out your illustrations."

My complete faith in John's intelligence allowed him to take me by the hand as a father leads his child, avoiding dangers and not losing my way by straying blindly into the unknown.

Only later did I appreciate how much he, in turn, relied on my skills. For the moment, I swallowed any resentment and listened attentively.

"The text is comprised of thirteen chapters, each on a different creature: the lion, the eagle, the serpent, the ant, the hare—my mind began to wander as he droned on adding another nine creatures. He had made his point sufficiently but nothing escaped him. "Asher! I hope you will pay attention. If we are to work to our best abilities, you must pray to the Lord to aid your concentration. Now listen! Each chapter is separated into two headings." He pointed at the Greek text and instantly translated it into Latin, "*Natura* and *Significacio*. The first part describes the beast. The second tells us the underlying moral allegory. Do you see?"

I nodded. That much was clear to me.

"This is how we will proceed. I will read the text to you in our language verse by verse. You will stop me to indicate where you wish to insert an illustration. I will write the Latin script, halt there and pass the vellum to you for your artwork. When you finish the image, we will continue with my writing. It will be slow and laborious, but I can think of no other approach." He looked at me and added out of politeness, "Unless you have a different idea, Asher."

I did not. I will spare no detail of that first morning. Now that the *Physiologus* is well known, it is much easier to see one of the many versions inspired by our success. I will only relate what we did with the lion. John bent over the ancient Greek text and began to recite with memorable ease that I still recall even as now he lies cold in his tomb. Thankfully, the Lord granted him a long life—ah, but my tired mind digresses. I concentrated on the words as he declaimed:

The lion stands on a hill, and when he hears a man
  hunting,
Or scents a man approaching,
By whatever way he will go down to the valley.
All his footprints he fills up after him;
He drags dust with his tail wherever he steps down—
Either dust or dew so that he cannot be found—
And hastens down to his den, where he may take refuge.

"Stop! Stop there!" I cried, "That will be my first illustra-tion, there."

"Very well. Now, I think I will write every heading or title in red ink." So saying, he dipped a quill in the crimson liquid before continuing in black. Whilst he scratched out the verse in his perfect minuscule script, I could visualise the scene of the lion crouching in his den. I would place the king of beasts in a rock grotto.

Soon, I was lost in thought—I had to decide on a policy for all the illustrations that I would be called upon to design. Ulti-mately, I decided to create a frame wherever there was to be a background. This surround would have a thick band of red and one of black separated by a narrow white line. Disregarding a background, I would depict figures without landscape directly against the vellum. John wrote slowly with infinite care, so that every letter was perfect and the spacing immaculate. It gave me time to continue my planning. Every picture would have an underlying sketch as a guide for me to paint over. But the colours would speak out. For instance, I could tint the sky to relate the time of day: dawn or sunset. As for shadows, they would principally be blue, and occasionally brown would serve. I would use light falling from an angle to create an effect.

"Oh, Asher." John's hand shook me from my reverie. "I've been trying to speak with you for some time. I see you are thinking about your work. Good! Well, I'm ready. I have finished the first verse; the ink is dry. Now it is your turn."

I took his place, squaring a frame with a straightedge before sketching inside it the outline of the den I had in my head, while he pored over the original text. No doubt he was already translating the next verse. I had to ignore his presence and concentrate. Thus, the lion slept with one eye open at rest within a cave, head upon its paws. It was time to paint: the sky I streaked with yellow, then red, before adding below a darker yellow tending gradually towards brown. The effect pleased me as it was clear I had evinced the coming night, which I made more apparent by a blue-white light striking the rocks of the cave from the left. Unaware of the abbey bells chiming the services, I did not notice John slip away for lunch. As ever, he respected my concentration, but thoughtfully returned with fresh bread and red wine for me.

"Do you like it?" I nodded towards my finished miniature, lacking only the final touch of the frame, a delicate task requiring a steady hand.

"It's perfect! You take a deserved break, Asher. Eat and drink. You can finish the surround when you are refreshed and I have reached the end of the page."

Latin presented no problem of comprehension to me. I followed the services in church without difficulty, so as I leant over John and understood his translation after my frugal lunch, I saw:

The Significance of the First Characteristic — written in red ink — then in black, I read:

Very high is that hill, which is heaven's kingdom;
Our Lord Christ is the lion, who lives above.
Oh! When it pleased our Lord to come down here to
*   earth,*

44

The devil did not know, though he hunts stealthily, and
   so forth.

I snorted; I had no intention of illustrating an interpretation
of the lion characteristic. For the first time, I realised the extent
of the task Archbishop Hincmar had given us. There were thirteen creatures, each with several characteristics and signifi-
cances to translate. Groaning inwardly, I foresaw that years of
work stretched before us. Admonishing myself, realising that
my gifts should unstintingly exalt the glory of God, I waited
patiently to learn the second characteristic of the lion. Even if I
peeked at the Greek writing, which I did, I could not understand it.

I must condense this tale of the *Physiologus,* suffice it to say
that work on the lion alone took us nearly three months. I
believe it a reasonable time when you consider the number of
miniatures I painted and the occasional setback, like when John
apologetically ripped up the page containing the scene of Jacob
blessing the lion of Judah because he had miswritten one word.
I understood his desire for perfection. Had I not done the same
to him because I did not like the antlers I had painted on a stag?

Working on this volume, I gained deeper insight into our
religion. Until then, I had not known why the lion represented
the Apostle, Mark. Now, every time I see a carving or painting
of a roaring lion in a church, I understand it symbolises the
Resurrection of Christ, the recounting of which tale is the main
purpose of that Gospel. Similarly, later, I learnt why the eagle
represents the Apostle, John, and so on.

The days in Hautvillers passed peacefully, in contrast with
the unreported horrors in the world outside our haven. One day
a small group of pilgrims recounted their narrow escape from a
roaming band of Norsemen. They told the brothers to beware
on account of how the Vikings targeted monasteries for trea-

sures as they were easy prey considering the helplessness of monks to defend themselves. They explained how these pagans had begun retaliatory raids after their defeat to Emperor Charles, who could no longer protect the towns and monasteries along the Seine. Farther inland, the heathens had plundered Chartres after rowing down the River Eure, a tributary of the Seine. The horror of that particular assault was that the savage Norsemen massacred the whole population of the town.

Their use of rivers was not lost on us as we pondered the situation of Hautvillers. Our monastery stood less than a mile from the River Marne, another tributary of the Seine. True, the trees of the forest ran down to its bank and screened the abbey. But, strangely, the notoriety of the relics of Saint Helena made us more vulnerable to attack.

Since John and I had some experience of warfare, we obtained an audience with the abbot, a spiritual monk, who preferred to put his faith in *the shield of God*. In his opinion, prayer would defend us. John's persuasive argumentation led to a more worldly decision, with the abbot placing us in charge of the defence of the abbey. We suspended work on the *Physiologus* and arranged for smiths to provide us with axes, spear tips, and arrowheads. These could be supplied in acceptable quantities, whereas sword-making required greater skills and too much time. John found and organised woodworkers to make hafts, shafts, and shields. His energy and organisational competence were outstanding.

Within three months, he had scheduled weapons training for the brothers. The abbot agreed to replace Terce, generally not an obligatory service, with mock fighting in the courtyard. The elderly monk looked on with mixed feelings as, day by day, the pacific monks transformed into a semblance of warriors. Competitive rivalry and camaraderie began to motivate them until, one day, John grinned at me and said, "We have a small army to defend our manuscript, Brother." His tone was exultant, but I had heard frightful tales of the battle skills of the Vikings. I feared that even the reinforcement of our palisades would not keep them at bay. Maybe our Father Abbot's reliance on prayer was not so misplaced. I admit, I dedicated my orisons to the deliverance of our abbey from the wrath of the Norsemen.

SIX

HAUTVILLERS, 858 AD

A rider in a state of panic informed the abbot that a Viking longship had entered the Marne: raiders would be upon the abbey within the day. The abbot, no less overwrought, immediately summoned John for advice.

"Oh, God help us! What are we to do?"

"There is much to do," John replied stoically. "Do I have your permission to organise the brothers, Father Abbot?"

"Ay, ay, anything! Do what you must."

My friend wasted no time, ordering every able-bodied man to drag dry twigs and branches from the forest. He had them create a long barrier in front of the monastery. Some grumbled, wondering how a low obstacle that a man could jump over might serve any purpose. But John knew what he was about; the pouring of oil over the brushwood revealed what he planned.

Back behind the barred gates, he had the monks take up their arms before lining them into several ranks. I recall to this day the ringing speech he delivered.

"Brothers, soon we will be under attack. I know many of you opted for a life of peace, but the Evil One has other ideas! I ask you to remember that these are not men you will be fighting against, but demons. Why else would they slaughter innocent women and babes? For every one you lay low, consider you are saving scores of innocents. God will smile upon you for this. Have no fear, because the Almighty is by our sides this day!"

This speech was greeted by a great roar and battering of weapons on shields as performed by real warriors. What John did not mention was their advantage of surprise, because the Norsemen expected either feeble fighters or no resistance. Overall, John had trained seventy-five monks. Even the elderly and overweight brothers prepared to lend a hand. A large pile of rocks, each the size of a man's head, was ready on the ramparts for them to hurl down on the foe. My friend had provided for this steady accumulation of boulders over the past few weeks. John called to the monks who had proved most accurate at the archery butts. He had them tie strips of linen to an arrow, which they then dipped in oil. Satisfied that the preparations were in place, all that remained was to wait.

The Vikings came streaming from the forest in their furs, faces painted with blue stripes, charging towards us with their round, coloured shields raised and their hoarse voices yelling fierce war-cries. The sight of them was enough to make the stoutest heart quake. John ordered the arrows lit and gave the command,

"Aim well at the barrier, tense your bows! Release!" He knew the timing was all-important.

Six flaming arrows struck the hurdle where the oil caught at once. Soon, a wall of flame sprang up before the advancing enemy. The careful timing meant that several of the advanced Norsemen were reduced to screaming and running away, their garments ablaze, as John had intended. It was the first warning that the monastery was not defended by feeble axe-fodder. The second came with a volley of arrows from the monks. True, the majority of the barbed arrowheads embedded in enemy shields, but at least four Vikings fell. Whereupon, John shouted, "There is only one ship's crew! We can destroy the heathen!"

A score of the foe took a running jump through the flames and rushed towards the wooden palisade. Their clear intention was to fight fire with fire. In moments, the abbey gates resembled a giant hedgehog, pierced by scores of flaming arrows. John, who had inspected the gates, was satisfied that they were made of oak trunks and knew that they could resist fire for hours. The Vikings, not knowing that, gathered their forces in front of the entry, as the scribe had hoped.

"Now!" he yelled at the elderly and unfit monks up on the ramparts. They hurled the heavy stones down on the unsuspecting Norsemen. Again, five foes dropped senseless to the ground. Not all the Vikings wore helmets. They raised their shields tardily. Six rocks thudded uselessly against the gaudily painted linden planks.

"Hold!" cried John. "And keep your heads down!"

He had seen two of the grey-bearded monks pierced by the arrows of Norse archers reacting to the rock attack. From the forest trotted six Vikings carrying a heavy looking tree trunk. John gathered a group of monks on the ramparts and issued two javelins each.

"See those men with the tree trunk? They have a ram to test the strength of our gates. At their first charge, rain the darts on them."

The Vikings had underestimated the preparation of the defenders. They disdained mere monks. On other occasions against a feared enemy, their chieftain would have protected the rammers with a shield wall. In their overconfidence, they paid the price as all six of the trunk bearers fell, impaled by one or more javelins. John organised another hail of rocks before deciding the time had come to take the offensive. In the court-yard, he lined us up in three ranks. There, in the centre of the first, I, a seasoned warrior, stood ready to lead the charge.

"Open the gates!" John bellowed while, like the wake of a boat, the acrid reek of smouldering arrows assailed our nostrils and the heavy barriers swung back.

"Charge!" I yelled, rushing forward, axe and shield at the ready. So swiftly had we exited the abbey that the Vikings had no time to organise a shield wall. I estimated that there were thirty of the formidable Norsemen. We were more than double their number.

"In the name of the Father!" I roared, crashing my axe with a jarring blow onto the shield of an adversary. As trained, the man next to me lunged his spear into the now unprotected belly of the warrior with his shield raised to protect himself from my strike. John's training had paid off straight away. Encouraged by this initial success, the other monks, with admirable discipline and armed with the confidence of superior numbers, pressed home our advantage. I searched in vain for a chieftain to take on, I might have known, he had already perished under John's unbridled assault. With his death, the Viking resistance, formidable but overwhelmed, broke. One by one, they turned to run for the forest. Sometimes we underesti-mate the capabilities of the elderly; from the ramparts hissed lethal arrows, many aimed badly, but some fatally striking the backs of the fleeing Norsemen.

It was now a question of hunting down fewer than ten men. John did not want any to escape. The victory was crushing: as far as I could tell, in the confusion of battle, we had lost no more than a dozen monks to the Vikings' blades. Each of those deaths strengthened our resolve to press on vengefully towards the river.

"This way!" John pointed to the moored longship. Sure enough, the survivors, shields abandoned for ease of running, were headed in that direction. I seized a javelin from one of the monks and, taking careful aim to the raucous cheers of my comrades, brought the last and nearest man to the ground, never to rise again. Following my lead, a dozen darts flew through the air. Only two struck home, but as John had declared in his rousing speech, every fallen enemy was the salvation of some innocent person elsewhere. A skeleton crew aboard the longship hauled their few defeated comrades over the gunwales and cut the ropes mooring the ship, which drifted to safety into the main current.

John seized a bow, strung an arrow, and found the thigh of a Viking who screamed useless curses at him. Soon, they were out of range.

The battle was over, for we could do nothing to prevent their escape. John expressed his disappointment to me. "They will inform their kinsmen and return. Next time, we will not have the advantage of surprise."

"You may be wrong, Brother John," I said without conviction, "they might prefer easier pickings. Most likely, they will inflate their tale to justify defeat. Along the lines that we had a giant monk in our ranks, with arms like a monster. That would be you!" We laughed partly in relief and also to keep up our courage.

The abbey was a strange place that evening as we conducted the funerals of the eight monks who had given their lives defending our home. Sorrow mixed with jubilation is a dizzying blend. Despite their emotions, the brothers, to their credit, managed to chant the solemn responses in the requiem.

Prayers over the graves, too, were conducted with tears and shared memories, but it is human nature to celebrate a victory and, commendably, after the burials, the abbot ordered a hogshead of wine to be consumed in the refectory. Divided among the whole community, it was a well-calculated amount: enough for raucous celebrations but insufficient to cause drunkenness.

During this, the abbot, who had never raised a hand in anger, called for order and began an oration.

"Brothers, this day, you have won a remarkable victory, praise the Lord! By the courage of your arms, you have preserved our monastery, its people and treasures intact. Let us spare another thought for our fallen brothers, whose sacrifice for our welfare will be remembered in our prayers at every service. I must especially commend Brother John, our scribe, whose military experience made the difference. Without his tactics, I dread to think of the horrors these walls might have witnessed."

He stood beaming upon his charges, paused to collect his thoughts, then thought it better to curtail his discourse.

"Enough of speechmaking and merriment, Brothers! We must retire to Compline and afterwards to a well-deserved night's sleep. As an exception, tonight, Matins and Lauds are not obligatory, for you have earned an undisturbed rest. However, I will expect to see you all at Prime." His blessing followed and relatively soberly, we trooped to the church.

On the way from the refectory to the chapel, John said to me, "Tomorrow, after Prime, we must organise the burning of the enemy corpses. The pagans are unworthy of Christian burial. To my knowledge, they cremate their dead and, in their heathen beliefs, their souls fly to the hall of their ferocious gods. As victors, we must at least grant them that, Asher."

For the time being, the operation of building an enormous pyre was John's last commitment as a military leader. With a jaundiced expression, he watched the crows flap away from the bodies when we disturbed their feasting.

"That speaks volumes about the futility of their religion, Brothers," came from between his clenched teeth. "The crow is their sacred bird. Even so, see how it pecks out the eyes of the dead! At least, *we* shall be spared the presence of Vikings in Heaven."

"Amen!" I cried as I hauled a heavy body near to the, as yet, unlit pyre. It took two of us to raise corpses into position. For the second time in twenty-four hours, John called for oil. Liberally sloshing it around the pyre, he instructed two brothers to touch their flaming brands onto the heap. In moments, flames leapt up to devour the crackling wood and the clothes and flesh of the thirty warriors.

John could not resist murmuring a prayer for the defeated enemy. "We must forgive them their blindness, for God, in His mercy, will judge each of them." When John had finished, he called the monks together in the courtyard. As he addressed them, many eyes were on the black pall of smoke beyond the palisade.

"Who among you was brought up in this area?"

Two hands raised hesitantly.

"The rest of you, return to your duties," he ordered. Not a man questioned his right to issue orders, so they left the four of us alone.

"What is it, Brother?" the older of the two monks asked.

"There must be a place nearby, some heights commanding a view of the river. Do you know of such a place?"

The monks exchanged glances, the younger nodded and muttered something about a standing stone.

"Ay, the lad is right, the hill of the menhir! Over yonder"—

his elder pointed south-west—"from there, the river stretches for leagues before the eye."

"What is your name?"

"Waldalenus."

"Brother Waldalenus, I am placing you in charge of our security. From now on, every day, a lookout must be placed on that hill with orders to warn of the impending arrival of a Viking ship. They will set out before Prime and return before the light fades."

"I will leave now. Tomorrow will be your turn, Brother Monegundis. While I am away, choose men for the next three days. Five of us should be sufficient—a watch every five days is not burdensome."

"Good idea. Also, take a horn with you. If Vikings are approaching, the sooner you warn us, the better!"

When we were alone, John confided in me. "I am weary in mind and body. I think we have earned a day to ourselves, Asher."

"As you say. I will speak with Brother Fardinanth. I doubt the amarius will object, under the circumstances."

Later, I found the elderly monk in a bad way: his frayed nerves were betrayed by a tic at the side of his eye. "What ails you, Brother?"

He stared at me with an anguished expression.

"Mea culpa, mea culpa, mea máxima culpa!"

But I was not his confessor. "What bothers you, Brother Fardinanth?" I took a step closer.

"Yesterday, I killed a man, Brother. I dropped a rock on his head."

"You helped to save the scriptorium from their flames, Brother. All our volumes are safe."

Had he not considered such a possibility? As if by magic, his face changed from anguish to relief. To drive home the cure,

I encouraged him. "Find the priest, Brother. Make your confession and you will feel better after absolution. Fear not, for in the eyes of the Lord, it was not murder you committed." I am not sure he heard my request for leave of absence as he hurried away, for he was hard of hearing.

John and I decided to wander into the woodland on the track to the river that we had hastened along in furious pursuit the day before. It was a splendid decision, as I adored the twittering of birds and the aroma of the herbs. The peace of the forest, broken only by the occasional rush of a squirrel or the clumsy flight of a jay, restored our spirits. I was telling John about the nervous state of Brother Fardinanth when he clutched my arm.

"Hush! Do you hear that?"

Some way off, down towards the river came the sound of voices.

"Don't worry. Those are not Vikings. Anyway, Brother Waldalenus has not sounded his horn."

John laughed and made a very pertinent remark. "I believe there is not a monk in the abbey today who is not shaken by the battle, myself included. I was worried on hearing those voices, wishing I had brought my axe and shield."

"They are probably harmless pilgrims. Soon, we will know."

My supposition proved wrong. No more than another twenty paces took us to a dishevelled, unkempt fellow holding a child's hand; behind him staggered a skinny, freckled woman with tousled red hair supporting on her arm an old man with a white beard, obviously exhausted.

"Brothers! Thank God! The monastery must be close," said the man in a thick, uncouth voice.

"Ay, a few hundred yards, but allow us to help," said John, picking up the boy who was maybe but four winters old, pressing him to his chest. "Best if you have a mule to give you a ride boy." The child giggled. "Brother Asher, relieve the woman of her father!" He had guessed correctly as the woman smiled her relief, saying, "Father, take the Brother's arm."

"Don't worry. It's not much farther to the abbey. There you can rest, eat and drink. Your strength will soon return." I ducked under his arm and hauled him to me, so that he now had more support. "That's better. Can you walk?"

He grumbled about his aches and pains as do the elderly all over the world. We hobbled along steadily, learning from their garbled account how they had escaped from their village set ablaze by Viking torches until the abbey gates came as a welcomed sight. I took the old man straight to the well where a tin cup of fresh water helped revive him as he sat gratefully on the stone wall surrounding it.

"Leave some for me, grandfather!" the child squealed.

"Don't worry, boy," John said. "Not even your grandfather can drink the well dry." The little fellow giggled again. Soon all four had slaked their thirst.

"Come, you must eat. You can finish your tale indoors," I said.

In the refectory, the younger man asked, "Where are all the soldiers?"

"What soldiers?" I asked.

"The German mercenaries who defeated the Norsemen."

Whilst I stared mouth agape, John understood in an instant. "Is that what they are saying? How people can start rumours! You are looking at your Saxon warrior, my friend."

Another mouth dropped open.

"Are you saying that you monks overcame the Vikings?"

"Thanks be to God, it is so!" He ruffled the boy's copper-blond hair distractedly. "Maybe, Brother," he said to me, thoughtfully, "these rumours will aid our cause. If the raiders think we have a troop of Saxons inside these walls, they will not venture up the Marne."

We all laughed and the boy, not understanding why, joined in with his giggles. It was the happiest we had felt since the panicked rider arrived.

SEVEN

HAUTVILLERS, 860 AD

The family of refugees was a forerunner to many other people fleeing from the Norsemen. Most of those drawn to seek a haven in our abbey were monks who had undergone harrowing experiences. The justified reputation surrounding the defensive capabilities of our monastery, undoubtedly inflated in the telling, made them hasten to us for refuge. Though we were secluded and out of touch with events in Frankia, John made it his business to interrogate each of the new brothers to piece together a clearer picture. What he learnt reflected little credit on our Emperor, Charles the Bald. Charlemagne had sapped Frankia's military strength, but the division of the Empire and the fighting between his grandsons for control of the middle kingdom worsened the situation. These circumstances further depleted the country's ability to defend itself against invaders.

One of the refugees, a middle-aged monk, earned himself the nickname of *Jonah* because some brothers, including John, heard his first declaration among us.

"I am a Jonah! Everywhere I go, ill-fortune pursues me."

The brothers, superstitious and narrow-minded, looked from one to the other with fear writ large on their faces. John first patiently extracted the monk's tale and then dispelled the nonsensical idea that the poor unfortunate brought bad-luck. I was not present at that interview, but this is what my friend told me.

"You should have seen them, Asher. Instead of pitying him for the terrible circumstances he found himself in, they allowed his silly outburst to fog their brains! Do you know, he escaped by a miracle from his monastery in Nantes? In reality, his wiry build saved him, for if he had been as rotund as one or two of our brothers, he would not have survived. It happened seventeen springs past when the Vikings sailed up the Loire to Nantes. That dreadful day, on the Feast of Saint John the Baptist, he was in the cathedral with the bishop and a small group of monks."

"What were they doing in the cathedral?"

"Asher, I hardly think that's relevant! Unlike you, I didn't ask."

I am often curious about minor details; it must be a defect or an attribute gained from my occupation as an illustrator. But I digress once more and rambling, I'm sure, is an unpardonable flaw. John continued his tale.

"Their first inkling that something was amiss came when the church bells sounded a wild alarm while warning horns blared. Our monk says that the bishop calmed them with pious words about the shield of God, but then the cathedral door burst open. The brother, with remarkable presence of mind when he saw the savage Vikings burst into the church, took advantage of the dim interior to dart unseen to a statue in a niche. His thin frame was slight enough for him to squeeze into the gap between the statue and the wall."

"That was quick thinking!"

"Indeed! From there, he witnessed the subsequent horrors. The bishop stood before the altar and commanded the Vikings to leave. They laughed in his face, and while some of the terrified monks ran hither and thither in vain, the Norsemen pursued and felled them with their axes. The cathedral echoed to their dying screams. As for the Bishop of Nantes, in an atrocious act of heathenry, the pagans manhandled him onto the altar, where they sacrificed him to his God."

"He died a martyr."

"In one sense, but he went as meekly as a lamb to the slaughter."

"Not everyone has your courage and fighting skills, John. Anyway, what happened to Brother Jonah?"

"That is *not* his name! He goes by Taurin—Brother Taurin. He spied on the fiends dripping blood, saw them leave the building with whatever bloodied treasures and jewels they could grasp. They did not find him, nor did they burn the cathedral, as they have done elsewhere."

"So, he was not so unlucky, after all."

"Exactly, Asher! Well said! You are not as credulous and stupid as the brothers who heard this tale. That is what I told them. Hark! Not only that but in Taurin's words, they then *perpetrated butchery of epic proportions* on the populace, sparing no one. He discovered this when after cringing, cramped and cold for a long time, he found the courage to emerge from hiding in the cathedral into the town where, to his horror, grotesque bloodied corpses lay strewn in the streets."

"And the Norsemen?"

"He discovered later that they sailed back with their plunder to the mouth of the Loire, to Noirmontier, a monastic island that they had seized as a base. Sadly, we can imagine the fate of the monks of that isle."

"You said this happened seventeen springs passed. So, where has the brother been since?"

"He tramped to Caudebec-en-Caux where, on the north bank of the Seine, stood the abbey of Saint Wandrille. The saint of that name founded it over two hundred years ago, but after a century of worship, a fire burnt it down. The monks rebuilt the monastery, but in January, eight years past, it burnt again, but this time it was no accident."

"The Vikings!" I exclaimed.

"You *are* quick-witted, Asher. The Brothers managed to escape with the relics of Saint Wandrille and gained temporary accommodation elsewhere. Brother Taurin, who, by the way, is a learned fellow, opted to march to the monastery of Tours, as we know, renowned for its library."

"Don't tell me the Norsemen attacked Tours!"

"Ay, they did, and destroyed the Saint Martin monastery. So, you see why our poor monk believes himself a Jonah. Yet he is alive to tell his tale. He also heard rumours that the Vikings are planning organised campaigns and wintering in the lower valley of the Seine. If this is true, there is little hope for the north. Taurin told me that many monks are attempting to move their archives and libraries to the south. The raiders have burnt several important libraries, Asher." He shook his head sadly, clicking his tongue.

Pausing for reflection, I ran my hand over my chin, enjoying the sensation of my beard tickling my hand. In those days, I always kept it short. Nowadays, as I repeat the same gesture while I dictate my tale to Brother Otmar, my palm runs over stubble because I no longer sport a beard. Oh, but I digress again, forgive me! After a moment, I said: "My God! All the work the scribes have put into those volumes only for them to end up as piles of ashes. What of our *Physiologus?* It doesn't bear thinking about!"

John's smile was grim.

"We haven't finished it yet, my friend. When we do, it would be safer here than in Reims. Yet, we are sworn to obedience and must take it and the original back to the Archbishop."

We spoke for a long time. Our conversation about the state of the kingdom became desperate as John added other tales of woe, gleaned from refugees to our abbey, who like Taurin hoped to be spared the merciless savagery of the Norsemen. Thus, I learnt of the sorry fate of other monasteries at their hands. Some occurred many years before, like the massacre at the destruction of the Church of Saint Martin the Confessor. More recently, John explained, the fiends had destroyed the monasteries of Saint Maixent, Charvoux, Saint Maur-sur-Loire, and Jumièges. The situation was grave and we both agreed that Charles the Bald needed to commit himself to serious counter-measures. Little did we foresee, that day, sunk in despair as we were, that the Emperor would indeed take the initiative, but his Edict was still four years away.

I believe that then we mooted our leaving Frankia for the first time. We considered returning to Fulda but agreed that, before long, the heathen would turn their attention to the rich Rhineland area. As it turned out, we were not wrong. We were, however, incorrect about our next destination after Hautvillers. But that is another story. I apologise, it is hard for my old brain to stick to the point. Much would happen before we arrived there almost a score of winters in the future.

We dedicated all our efforts to completing the *Physiologus* and, at last, the great day arrived when I finished my last illustration, relating to the *Significance of the Mermaid*. Our provisioner convinced us that Reims would produce a superior binding. We accepted his argument and betook ourselves to the abbey and an audience with Archbishop Hincmar.

He was delighted with our achievement and spoke to us

about the contact he had begun with a young prince in Anglia, an island to the west of Frankia. This young man was *extremely cultured* and had *an unparalleled thirst for learning* in the pompous words of the Archbishop. The son of the late King Aethelwulf of Wessex, Alfred.

"He will make a great king," said Hincmar prophetically, "and I am minded to gift him your Physiologus. After all, *I* have the original Greek version," he crowed. Inwardly, I felt offended. How could that shabby old manuscript stand comparison with our masterpiece? Still, who were we to argue? Neither of us had heard the name of this Alfred until that day, nor did we imagine ... but stay! I am about to digress again. Back to my tale—my thought on that occasion was that the young prince, from the words of Hincmar, was a more than worthy recipient of our treasured volume.

The Archbishop had not finished with surprises. Turning to John, he asked, "So, how is Gottschalk?"

John and I exchanged glances of bafflement, but the prelate chortled.

"You know nothing of the heretic, do you? I really must commend your abbot on his discretion. Gottschalk, a reprobate, has been securely held at Hautvillers for, let me see, *um,* eleven years. Ay, for the Council at Querzy was convened in 849—how time flies!"

John's curiosity got the better of him. "Eleven years! Who is this heretic and what has he done?"

"What hasn't he done? That might be a more pertinent question. I will concede a few details," Hincmar said magnanimously. "Gottschalk first came to our attention in 829, when as a young monk in Orbais, he took out a lawsuit against his abbot. He claimed that they tonsured him violently against his will. The tribunal pronounced in his favour. Somehow, he managed to become ordained as a priest and then began spouting his theories about predestination."

I will not weary you with the Archbishop's theological exposition, suffice it to say that Gottschalk drew his theology about grace from a long-forgotten doctrine of the Church Father, Augustine. When my acute-minded friend pointed this out to Archbishop Hincmar, the prelate was nonplussed. John, as brave in debate as on the battlefield, not content, went on to suggest, "This former priest's views contravene the Emperor's claims to divine favour. Since we live in times of rebellion and civil war, which draw people away from traditional Frankish religious teachings, dear Archbishop, his words sound, I repeat, *sound* like heresy."

Hincmar's countenance, at first thunderous, cleared, but he frowned in concentration. "You make a very good point, Brother John. Yet, leading ecclesiastics at the Synod of Mainz convicted him and had him beaten and exiled from the territories of Louis the German, never to return. They handed him to me. My reaction was to return him to his former monastery of Orbais. But as the Book of Proverbs says, *Just as a dog returns to its own vomit, so a fool reverts to his folly.*"

"Proverbs 26:11," I heard John mutter. So did the Archbishop.

"Exactly, my learned friend," he muttered. "So, the madman demanded his sentence should be overturned. Hence, we finished up before the Emperor at Querzy where he attempted again to justify his ideas. Once more, he was condemned as a heretic, scourged and obliged to burn his declaration of faith."

The Archbishop's brow wrinkled while his eyes narrowed and became hard.

"Do you know, he prayed to be allowed to prove his doctrine

in a deadly ordeal modelled after an ancient martyr tale: he would climb in and out of barrels of boiling water, oil, lard, and pitch only to emerge miraculously unscathed thanks to divine protection. We bishops would be revealed as reprobate heretics, not him. As you know, we accept ordeals as a way of establishing criminal guilt or innocence in our Empire, but Gottschalk's claims that a miraculous event would prove his orthodoxy are unprecedented. Suffice it to say, the ordeal was seen as further evidence of his heretical vanity and madness—we could not permit such a thing."

For such a confident man, I noticed the hesitation as the Archbishop looked somewhat abashed at John.

My friend seized the initiative with, "And since then, the poor soul has been hidden from humanity in a cell."

"My idea," said the Archbishop, "is that you, Brother John, should visit him frequently, under my authorisation. Attempt to understand him and determine whether his mind is infected by heresy or not. Meanwhile, you have both completed the *Physiologus* so wonderfully well that I have another task for you. I require a psalter, but no ordinary volume."

I groaned inwardly; he continued.

"One suitable for the visual education of the monks. Brother Asher, your illustrations must capture the spirit of each psalm, verse by verse. You, John, will have to work on a larger scale, as the tutor will display the volume to the onlooking novices."

"I see," said John thoughtfully. "Then, perhaps I could return to an older, more legible script than our current minuscule."

The prelate beamed. "I will leave those details to your judgment. That will be all for now. Bless you both for the splendid work you have done. Oh, Brother John, my heartfelt thanks for repelling the heathens at Hautvillers. The Emperor,

JOHN THE OLD SAXON

I know, wishes to reward you, although I know not what he has in mind."

We bowed our way out. On the return journey to our abbey, John said to me, "You know, Asher, it is as well the Archbishop authorised me to visit the prisoner, because I would have done so anyway."

Knowing my friend, of this I had no doubt. What I could not have known then was how important to our future this Gottschalk, unknown to us, would prove to be.

EIGHT

Our abbot displayed doubt when we told him of our authorisation to visit Gottschalk. After all, he had kept his presence secret from everyone except three trusted brothers sworn not to breathe a word. Reluctantly, he allowed us to enter the small cell, where we saw that the prisoner had a table, parchment, quills and ink.

Understandably, he leapt to his feet at the sight of new faces and his sallow features lit up with joy. When we told him our names, he surprised us by saying, "I know you both. You were at Fulda when I was a novice under Abbot Rabanus Maurus."

The realisation that this man had the nerve to take out a lawsuit against our formidable former abbot shocked me. What gall! His claim that this learned and benevolent monk was responsible for a forcible tonsuring struck me as absurd, so I searched his face for signs of cunning, but his pale-grey eyes reassured me he was shrewd, not crafty.

By his admission, he had written missives to defend his views to many eminent theologians in the lands of Charles the Bald and Louis the German. Proudly he showed John, whom I presume he had singled out as the more intellectually gifted of the two of us, letters from five theologians penned in his favour, wherein he expounded his doctrine of two-fold predestination. I will spare you the intricate details of the argument by simply stating he believed in predestination by God to condemnation *and* salvation.

For those against his views, two episodes from his past further exasperated and sparked the controversy.

"People take me less seriously because I am labelled a renegade monk. Even when I became a priest, my bishop would not consecrate me, so I had to turn to Rigbold, the chorepiscopus of Reims, to perform the ceremony, a kindly soul who bore me no grudges."

"So, how did you manage to overcome your problems in Frankia?" I asked.

He threw back his head and laughed, which seemed so out of place in the confined space of his cell.

"I crossed the border into Italy where I found a patron in Verona and, later, in the Margrave of Friuli." He could see I was impressed, and added, "That was only the beginning of my travels, which took me into Dalmatia, Pannonia, where the Magyars live, and Noricum. I will tell you about my wanderings if you come to me again, but for now, I wish to speak about my beliefs."

John did not surprise me with his knowledge and grasp of theology. Indeed, he countered some of Gottschalk's arguments by quoting from memory passages written by our Archbishop Hincmar in his *De Praedestinatione* penned precisely to refute the prisoner's heresy. For a while, Gottschalk became defensive, but realising that John had not come in aid of Hincmar, he spoke about his attempts to have an equitable hearing at the Council of Valence these five years passed. Unsuccessful, he wrote and pleaded for another hearing, which took place at Savonnières just a twelvemonth ago.

"How could I obtain a fair hearing when they were more concerned with Louis the German's invasion and Charles's condemnation of the treacherous Archbishop Wanilo of Sens? Did you know that Hincmar wrote Charles's long and successful censure of that prelate? Do you suppose, then, that Hincmar would not have the ear of the Emperor after that?" Gottschalk sighed and momentarily despaired before his countenance hardened into resolve.

"But I *will* be heard! The theologians I mentioned earlier are pursuing my case with the Holy Father in Rome."

I mention this conversation, only because it has a bearing on our future lives.

For the moment, John replied, "You have a stronger case than what the Frankish episcopate are prepared to accept. Who knows?"

At this, the poor prisoner sprang across his cell and took John in an embrace. "Bless you for your words, Brother! They give me hope."

John extricated himself and said, "We will return to speak further on the matter."

Thus began our weekly visits, in which we discovered that the captive not only wrote letters but had notebooks full of poems and sketches. I make no bones about it: I drew upon that artwork for our psalter, which later became so famous. Not only that, I had him sketch me scenes from his travels, which I borrowed to enhance our manuscript. Before coming back to the conditions of Gottschalk, I wish to explain the psalter.

Archbishop Hincmar made his requirements clear. Based on requiring an instructional psalter for a group of novices to gather round to gaze at and learn by heart, John opted to abandon the minuscule script used throughout our *Physiologus* in favour of the older style Rustic Capitals— an excellent choice. Inspired by Gottschalk's sketches, I chose to draw in bistre, a decision John accepted eagerly and he, too, adopted the same medium. When we finished our work, we had filled one hundred and eight vellum leaves, which measured thirteen by ten inches, the pages formed by quires of eight pages folded.

Since the Archbishop had demanded a lively and original work, what better way than to adopt the mannerisms of the captive's sketches? I must say that he showed a liveliness of mind and by taking from him, I obtained the independence from conventions that Hincmar sought. The novelty of my creation not only resided in the number of illustrations required, because I needed to illustrate each verse, but also in the size of the manuscript and the large groups of small figures I depicted without the use of frames. The psalter became highly influential in scriptoria throughout the West, especially in the land we were later to call our home.

John cautioned me with a sardonic smile, "Asher, be sure not to mention to the Archbishop whence your innovation came!"

Of course, I never did. I am ashamed to say that I claimed all the merit. But as John stated, "You had the inspiration to make use of drawings not intended for the purpose. The psalter is wholly to your credit, Asher."

That much was true; but I will give one example from the one hundred and sixty-six illustrations I produced: Psalm 115. The drawing depicts the Psalmist, identifiable by the bands around his arms as in verse 7, standing below the crucified

71

Christ. The weight of Christ's body pulls down on his arms, his head rests on his right shoulder, and his eyes are closed in death. David lifts the chalice to catch the blood flowing from Christ's side. In the other hand, he holds out a paten with the eucharist bread toward an altar.

I had never seen a similar illustration until I saw it sketched in Gottschalk's notebook.

"How did you come up with this idea?" I asked, barely unable to contain my excitement.

"I copied it from, let me see," he hesitated, stroked his chin, then remembered, "in Noricum, a place called Munich. Ay, I'm sure it was there on the ivory cover of a collection. I think a volume of *Pericopes*. When I see something I like, even for a second, I memorise it and can sketch it later."

He had a remarkable talent. My portrayals were never identical, but his sketches inspired me. John, meanwhile, had discovered that beyond the man's obsession with predestination, there was an acute brain filled with considerable learning.

"Asher, it is a pity that Fulgentius should rot in that cell when he has so much to offer."

"Wait! What did you call him?"

John's beard bobbed with his laughter. "It's a nickname that his friend Walahfrid Strabo settled on him after Fulgentius the Mythographer, whom he studied intensely. You see, Asher, the man is a goldmine of knowledge. That's the pity of it."

"I do believe, John, that you are befriending a heretic."

"Well, you see, I'm not so convinced of his heresy."

"Beware, my friend, it is a dangerous path you would tread."

John gazed at me thoughtfully, put one hand in the other and said, "The poor fellow is a Saxon, like us. His father, like ours, was a Count, named Bernius. You know, his situation makes me feel that, but for fortune, I might be in his position."

"Nay, John, you exaggerate! It is Gottschalk's character that has resulted in his imprisonment. A man like you is wise enough to keep his mouth shut; the prisoner is not."

"Are you saying that we should punish a man for his beliefs, Asher?"

"Not for them, but for bandying them around to all and sundry in the wrong places."

Our argument continued for a long time. I believe it to have been one of the most heated of our entire friendship. In the end, it had no importance since events moved unstoppably forward.

A messenger from Archbishop Hincmar brought a letter for John in May 863. The Pope, Nicholas I, had summoned Hincmar to a Council to be held in Metz the following month. The missive from the Archbishop explained to John that he was to go in his place to discuss the case of Gottschalk and his supposed heresy, among other political matters. John, provided with an armed escort, would accompany the heretic—as the Archbishop insisted on calling him—who would defend himself before the Pope.

John's absence from Hautvillers to attend the Council was the longest period of separation in our enduring friendship. Not that his measured and less than wholehearted support of Gottschalk helped much, because nothing changed in the prisoner's situation.

That in itself changed ours though. Gottschalk sank into depression, his spirit was broken, from which he never recovered.

Any scribe will tell you that the passing of time becomes unreal. Ay, it can be measured in manuscripts completed, but a life dedicated to the glorification of God through the written word or drawn image requires a very fixed and limited horizon. The metronomic life of the monk, governed by church bells calling the brothers to the offices meant our eyes briefly traversed the courtyard and the nave while the seasons inexorably passed us by. Occasionally, I would realise with a start that I had not seen a tree in months, let alone enjoyed the sensation of running my hand down its rough bark. In such a moment, my soul ached for wide-open spaces —the vision of a mountain range or the ocean on my skyline. We were living in a suspended state since John, more than I, had decided some time ago to leave the abbey, but circumstances conspired, allowing the seasons to sneak by like thieves in the night. Thus, a year became a decade and we were still, to my friend's exasperation, within the same monastic walls while the wider world called to us with a sweet siren song.

In that period of seven years, we finished the psalter and presented it in Reims to the delighted Archbishop, whose praise was lavish. He particularly praised the illustration for Psalm 27, centred on *they that go down to the pit.* I had drawn winged figures that prick the *workers of iniquity* with spears. On the left, a king stands before a temple; Christ and his angels are shown above. Perhaps the Archbishop liked the originality of the umbrella held over the king—something unknown in the West—again thanks to Gottschalk's inspiring sketchbook.

Our feelings for Hincmar were not reciprocal, because in 868 Gottschalk became gravely ill. How shocking to see the weight fallen off his frame and his sallow face, now skeletal, peered at us in despair. The Archbishop refused John's plea to allow the prisoner outdoors into the fresh air he so badly needed and, when he fell critically sick, Hincmar denied him the sacraments unless he recanted his views. The theologian died alone in October, and to make matters worse, Archbishop Hincmar refused to allow his burial in consecrated ground.

In all our years, I have not seen John so sickened.

"We must leave this place! I cannot serve a moment longer under this so-called Man of God!"

Despite John's understandable anger, I believe the reason we did not depart on the instant was that we had only just started a new sacramentary intended for the Archbishop's personal use. This was an important assignment comprising the pre-Gregorian three parts, corresponding to the liturgical year, made up of masses for Sundays and feasts, prayers, rites and blessings of the Easter font and the oil, and prayers at the dedication of churches and the reception of novices. Adding to this the frontispiece I had to produce, it became a considerable task that would take at least two years to complete.

Our decision not to leave at once was reinforced by the Edict of Pîtres, 864, by which the Emperor finally reacted strongly to the Viking raids. This set of laws promised so much. We hoped that the safety of the kingdom had been secured and that remaining at Hautvillers would provide us with the peaceful setting we craved to produce our masterpieces. The purpose and primary effect of the Edict was to be the protection of the cities and countryside from Viking raids. Charles created a large force of cavalry upon which he could call as needed. He ordered all men who had horses or could afford horses to serve in the army as cavalrymen. The Emperor intended to have a mobile force with which to descend upon the raiders before they could up and leave with their plunder. Also, the Edict stipulated that the penalty for selling horses to the Vikings was death.

In our secluded monastery, in 871 news reached us of the demise overseas of King Aethelred and the succession of Alfred, the prince who had received our *Physiologus*. We did not give the matter much thought at first, but as we neared the end of the sacramentary for Archbishop Hincmar, an invitation arrived from King Alfred of Wessex.

The letter, couched in his hand, laid out his intention to gather learned men to his court in Winchester to spark a revival of learning throughout his kingdom. I knew at once that John intended to set sail for Anglia. I was not so enthusiastic. Besides, news came that Angle-land was under attack from the Great Heathen Army. I feared that having saved our monastery in Hautvillers and enjoyed years of peaceful scribing, as a result, we would now plunge headlong into another Viking slaughterhouse.

"Look here, Asher, my mind is set. I leave for the coast tomorrow. I will find a ship to take me to Angle-land. Give me a farewell kiss if you are not coming with me. I promise I will write to you frequently. This is too good an opportunity to let slip."

We might as well have been siblings born of the same mother, not just brothers in vows: so, how could I watch him walk away? For the sake of shameful petty satisfaction, for some hours, I let him think I would stay in Hautvillers. The sight of his miserable face made me relent. In his unbounded joy at my apparent change of heart, he almost broke my ribs with his enthusiastic hug.

"Asher, I knew you would come!"

"I can always change my mind again. Anyway, we should remain to celebrate Christ's Mass and wait for the spring. I have no wish to visit the seabed on a perilous storm-tossed voyage."

In our years together, this was the only concession I can remember obtaining from him. So, we waited until the winter had passed and the gentler breezes of spring wafted us on our way over what sailors insisted was a crossing of seven leagues. At last, I had my longed-for open horizons, not that I could enjoy them. That distance did not seem so far but, I swear, I vomited once for each league of the voyage. Typically, John did not suffer from the *mal de mer*. Now that I am old and comfort-able in our English abbey, I can say that my suffering was worthwhile. Had you asked about my feelings on that rolling ship, my reply might not have been befitting of a Benedictine monk.

NINE

Our arrival in Angle-land armed with an invitation from the King of Wessex to his court was confusing, to say the least. We soon discovered that his Kingdom was the last bulwark against the Scandinavian onslaught. Even Wessex was teetering and on the verge of collapse. We did not realise this, because our assumptions were so far removed from the reality of King Alfred's situation.

By the midsummer of 877, we arrived at the royal palace in Winchester where we expected to find a welcoming monarch on his throne. Instead, we found taut-faced servants of various ranks, who informed us that the King was away fighting the Norsemen. If we supposed that he was dealing with a band of Norse raiders, we soon learnt otherwise. Messengers came and went, and although the news filtered through to us in dribs and drabs, we heard that a fearsome Viking chieftain named Guthrum, at the head of the Great Heathen Army, was threatening the existence of the Kingdom of Wessex. The fighting was intense around a city called Exeter. One day, the messengers were confident of a Saxon victory; the next, they spoke in sorrowful terms of another hard-fought defeat. If my memory serves, there were four great battles after which the weakened Alfred survived to fight again, but the omens for the future of his throne were grim.

The onset of winter saved him from likely defeat. Guthrum's retreat to Gloucester where the Viking horde would stay during the harsh season seemingly spared the exhausted Saxons.

One morning, a messenger arrived from King Alfred. I spotted a man, his cloak and beard dripping rainwater, talking with a monk. Suddenly, the brother pointed in our direction, at which the newcomer clapped him on the upper arm and hastened towards us.

"John and Asher of Saxony?" he inquired with a tone of expectancy.

As usual, John spoke for the two of us. "Ay, who is it that wants to know?"

"Brothers, I come from the King. I bear this missive for your eyes only."

The messenger reached inside his tunic and withdrew a folded letter sealed with red wax that he handed to John. Not hesitating to admire the waxen imprint, as I would have done, John broke it open and began to read aloud for my benefit. After all these years, I cannot bring to mind the exact wording, but the gist was an apology for not receiving us at Winchester. I remember this much: *we have been otherwise engaged*. I recall thinking that in these words he made light of his desperate fight for survival. But I digress once more, for he invited us to go forthwith to Chippenham for the celebration of Christ's birth.

Although it was where King Alfred's sister wed Burghred, King of Mercia, twenty-five years previously, neither of us had any knowledge of the place. John stated as much, but the messenger replied that he was charged with providing us with horses and arms, so that he might conduct us safely and rapidly to the royal vill of Chippenham. Little did I imagine that I would test the newly acquired sword in such a manner, but more on that later. My memory of the ride to Chippenham is that of spattering mud and drenching rain. I recall the sight of a swollen river, its rapid current careening past us as we rode along its eastern bank to where the warmth of the royal palace awaited us. Our companion, surprised at the surge, told us it was the Avon, the same that ran through Bath and thence to Avonmouth.

A group of five scholars, who had waited all day impatiently for our arrival, reserved a welcome for us. The fame of our manuscripts had preceded us to Wessex. It was not scholarly exchange we craved but hot water and dry clothes. The most perceptive of the small band, a Briton named Asser—we laughed about the similarity of our names; it was how I acquired the name Gwyn—sensed our discomfort and provided these essentials.

"I'm going to call you Gwyn, brother. Our names are too alike. Your name translated into my language is Gwyn: it means *Blessed*. I have admired your handiwork, so the name is most apt, Brother Gwyn."

That name, given with affection, has remained with me all my life. It took John some months to accustom himself to it, but soon he was calling, "Brother Gwyn, don't you agree?" and such like.

Anyway, the Welshman led us, now dry, comfortable, and presentable, to meet our new patron. I liked him, but he did not join the King's court permanently until eight years later—even then, he took some persuading. More about Asser later, for I must recount our first meeting with King Alfred. I had heard accounts of his exploits as a warrior-King, so I was expecting a mighty, muscular warrior. Instead, before his throne stood a slender figure of medium height. The blond hair and beard framed a face of acute intelligence where piercing blue eyes twinkled with wit and good humour. He repeated his apology expressed in the letter, but with a self-irony that, speaking strictly for myself, conquered me immediately.

When he proceeded to eulogise our work but without a trace of flattery, I knew that we were dealing with an exceptional ruler. My first impression, shared with John, as he later confessed, was of a pious and earnest King, who lectured even his learned clerics on the finer points of their profession. Alfred was a lover of wisdom, who knew the Bible thoroughly and often quoted it as a guide to spiritual life. All of this was apparent to us on our first encounter but, successively, as the day of Christ's Mass approached, we learnt that he was a King who believed in the Providence that had raised him improbably to the throne. He came over as a warrior-king and pious scholar who understood these two aspects of his life as complementary, based on his Christian duty as a man and as a ruler. Within ten days of knowing him, I swear I would have followed him willingly even into the flaming maws of Hell. Such was the force of his personality that inspired devotion in the breast of each man surrounding him.

Alfred had invited us to participate in the festivities to celebrate Our Lord's birth. Both John and I expected lavish banqueting. Imagine our surprise to find the King and his courtiers fasting. It was mid-winter, there was no work in the fields, the food stored in granaries was lost to the raiders or had to be saved to tide folk over the harsh months. Oh, he feasted all right, but on the day the Church recognised as the anniversary of Christ's birth, the twenty-fifth day of the month. Even then, his solemn rejoicing set the tone at his high table where serious discussion held sway on the meaning of the tale told in the

Gospels. The King ignored the rowdy, traditional wassailing of his warriors seated below us in the body of the hall. Indeed, like a benevolent father, he raised his drinking horn to toast them several times, always with a smile on his face.

In our more serious discussions, the lilting accent of Asser predominated. We admired his intellect and learning, realising how beloved of the King was this monk from St David's in Dyfed. King Alfred, voices whispered, had begged the scholar at some length to join him at his court. More about him later in my tale, but suffice it to say that his exchanges with John raised the discussion to levels that delighted the monarch, who interrupted occasionally to clarify this or that theological point. His esteem for John grew to match that in which he held Asser. Of course, John would supersede Asser in a field the Briton knew nothing about—more on that later.

I sometimes wonder whether the Vikings, knowing something of our faith, had sent a spy to verify the drunkenness and revelry that they associated with their wild festivities. How else can what followed be explained? They must have known that the Twelfth Night was important in our religion, marking as it does the end of the Christmas celebrations. They brought death, not Epiphany gifts. The royal vill at Chippenham was fortified, so on the eve of Twelfth Night, in the morning, warning horns blared from the ramparts while the church bells sounded the alarm. John and I ran to our quarters and retrieved our swords. We had no armour and no fear. With ne'er a thought, we joined King Alfred's warriors and hastened into the courtyard.

The gates were already resounding to the thuds of a battering ram. The Saxon defenders lined up in disciplined shield-wall facing the gate, which ceded to the blows even as we gazed on in dismay. In poured the ferocious Danes in overwhelming numbers. They charged forward with fierce cries, their round, gaudily-painted shields raised. A generally shaggy appearance, long hair tied or plaited back, unkempt beards and fur stoles brought the image of a teeming wolf pack to my mind. Miraculously, the shield-wall held against the full force of the onslaught. John forced his way to the King, watching the battle amid his bodyguard, hand-picked warriors chosen for their valour. They had not yet entered the fray as the King weighed his options.

"Sire," urged John, "is there another gate? You must flee if you are to live to fight again." He did not wait for an answer, but added, "We should hasten to the stables, the better to escape the wrath of the Vikings."

The King, quick-witted as ever, hesitated only to assure himself of the presence of Asser before we turned in an orderly fashion to gain the horses so that a score of warriors and a handful of scholars, including the Welshman, rode out through a postern gate. Naturally, the Norsemen had stationed a reserve to guard that exit, but we hacked through them, John showing he was the equal of any of Alfred's chosen men. I accounted for three Vikings before we completed our escape.

John, with no idea whither the road led, drew alongside the King's steed. "Sire, I know not this land, but is there a place we may encamp to hold against greater numbers?"

"Ay, there is such a place we can reach once we come to Bath." In that town, King Alfred gathered another score of warriors and, choosing a guide, had him lead us to the ancient fortress—its origins lost in the mists of Time—Badbury Rings. The Britons of yore who had constructed the hillfort had dug deep concentric ditches. With fatigue, we reached the enclosure of the upper ring. At a guess, the top was over three hundred feet above the level of the sea.

The King, whose learning ever surprised me, spoke thus: "Brother Gwyn, a British tribe called the Durotriges built this fortress before the Romans came to our land. Did they not choose the site well?"

"Ay, Sire, they did," I said. "We can hold this position until our water runs out."

"Nay, Brother, we shall spend but one night here."

That was when John joined in, bringing his military expertise to bear on our situation.

"Sire, I wish to relate our experience with the Vikings when we were in Frankia ..." He went on to tell Alfred how we had destroyed the enemy longship at the Abbey of Hautvillers. I was surprised, because John never spoke without purpose or merely to vaunt his achievements. But, then, all became clear.

"So, you see, Sire, if I may presume to offer military counsel to a warrior-king ..." He paused and waited for the royal assent, which came in the form of an enigmatic smile and a nod. "Well, we need to find an *impregnable* defensive position whence you can steadily raise your forces by sending messengers to muster warriors from around your Kingdom. But, before finding such a haven, any hiding place will suffice until we find its ideal location. This fortress cannot supply the food and water we need, and it is too exposed."

"You are right, Brother John. I had thought the Forest of Selwood, which provides a great natural obstacle and lies on the frontier between the east and west of my Kingdom, would serve as a temporary hiding place. Did you have a forest in mind?"

John shook his head. "Nay, but, Sire, that will suffice for our immediate safety and supply us with food and warmth." I swear he shivered as he pulled his cloak tighter around him, for the late-afternoon air was keen on that hilltop.

Springing to his feet, Alfred organised four lookouts to be relieved in turn throughout the night. "If all is clear after the dawn, we leave for Selwood," the monarch stated.

I admired the calm determination in his voice, little imagining that it was from here that the Saxon resurgence would begin. If we lived to tell the tale, it is thanks to the doughty warriors massacred at the royal vill of Chippenham. I often wonder whether Guthrum's greatest mistake was to let us slip out of his grasp. Maybe that will become clear as my narrative unfolds. Also, how strange that two Saxons from Old Saxony should have been instrumental in the survival of New Saxony, the Kingdom known as Wessex.

TEN

Selwood Forest, winter, 878 AD

Our first foray out of the forest was enforced following scouts' reports of a planned Viking raid on Shaftesbury. This hilltop settlement near the Wiltshire border vaunted a flourishing minster church, which doubtless attracted the Norsemen, ever thirsting for treasure. We split our forces into three separate encampments within a radius of two leagues for better concealment and rapid reaction.

Assembling the men of our camp, King Alfred told us news of the Viking incursion.

"One of our spies has revealed that a force of Norsemen is on its way to Shaftesbury. They intend to sack the minster church. We must ride out at once and give them a taste of Saxon steel. My man tells me their number is that of two longship crews—four-score warriors. We can deal with them if we move quickly."

"Sire, should we not rouse the other two camps?" I asked.

"Nay, Brother Gwyn, we shall waste no time. To the horses!"

John later told me, after Alfred had confided in him, that his intention to defeat the Danes with an equally-matched force was to serve as a message to wavering Saxons that the Norsemen could not sweep all before them. If that was his plan, it succeeded.

We galloped out of the forest and headed for Shaftesbury, easily seen standing high on its hill at, I'd say, some 750 feet above the level of the sea. We were in time because, as we approached, we saw the Danish force on foot, toiling up the slope towards the town. Our horses were fresh, so we eagerly urged them on.

"Axe, Gwyn!" John commanded tersely, but I didn't hear his words lost in the thundering beat of hoofs. It mattered not, because I had decided to favour my axe over the sword since we had the benefit of height from the saddle: a form of battle unknown to us. On previous occasions we had dismounted and fought on foot. This time, King Alfred insisted that there was no value in throwing away the advantage of height and mobility. How right his words proved.

We were upon the advancing Norsemen before they had time to form into their impressive shield-wall. True, we lost several horses to their blades, but fighting on horseback was telling. I, alone, crashed my axe into the necks of four raiders. John, a better horseman and fiercer warrior, accounted for double that number. The victory was swift, so that our triumphant King rode with a swagger into the town where the priests and the more prominent men of the place greeted him.

The townsfolk celebrated with an improvised meal. I cannot call it a feast, because it was simple fare that restored our spirits and tired limbs. Before eating, King Alfred insisted on prayer in the minster church to thank God for our victory. After the service, he climbed the tower to admire the view stretching to the horizon, embracing the tor at Glastonbury.

"Do you know, John, I am minded to build an abbey in this place. Do you not think that with stout fortifications Shaftesbury would hold out against the fiercest foe?" said our King.

"Sire, when we defeat Guthrum, you would be wise to fortify many burghs around the Kingdom for when the heathen regroups."

"John, I like your optimism! But never have we been so weak: our situation is dire. Today's exploit is a message I send to my people to find their courage and take up arms. We shall speak of this at the table," he said, gazing once more at the magnificent view from the windswept tower top. I was happy to regain the winding stairs to set foot on level ground.

The time has come in this narrative to introduce John's nemesis, Brother Esegar. This monk, at a guess, no older than us, was to prove a thorn in our side for many years, as I will relate.

The second son of a Wessex ealdorman, from the start he resented us, not only as outsiders but the more as foreigners. Many of his expressions, gestures, and words revealed burning jealousy of John's esteem on the part of the King. Only a blind man would not have noticed his reactions. In his favour, Brother Esegar was a capable scholar, learned both in Latin and Greek. He was also a sociable fellow: his quick wits and humour made him a popular companion. But, more to the point, he was only affable like that with those whom he favoured. Needless to say, those fortunate souls were exclusively West Saxons unless he had some underlying purpose. John and I were not among his confidants, although he loved arguing with John on theological matters, especially if the King was within earshot. It soon became clear to me that this Saxon monk, more than anything else, sought to gain the esteem of our monarch. I ascribe this to his family background.

Esegar, as the second son, could not hope to claim his

father's title or estates, but from what I gathered, would have settled for his affection. The nobleman denied him fondness, too, making him resentful especially since he had no strong vocation for the monastic life which they forced upon him. To his credit, he emerged from his cloistered boyhood with a reputation as a scholar. I feel sure that this was due to his natural intelligence and curiosity rather than any devotion. The early death of his mother drove him, as a boy, to seek his father's approval, but that nobleman, engaged in a battle for survival against the savage Norsemen, like his King, could spare little time for the youth. On the contrary, his father dedicated much effort to training his eldest son in arms and encouraging his involvement in the estates.

Consigned to the monastery at Wilton, Esegar swore that he would make his father proud. To a remarkable extent, he made rapid progress—by his early thirties, he had achieved notoriety beyond the gates of his monastic home. Thus, he had come to the attention of the King, whose earnest desire to surround himself with scholars led to a similar invitation as ours to the court.

At the table that evening, as was his right, Alfred began the discussion.

"We have won a battle today, but take care with exultation, for victory and prosperity depend upon royal obedience to the divine will. Is it not so, my friends?"

Brother Esegar almost choked on a crust of bread in his eagerness to be the first to reply and ingratiate himself with his King. "Quite so, Sire, and you are an example to us all. Only one who is humble and strong in heart is ready for such great responsibility."

There was a quiet moment as we deliberated these fine words. Nor did the King say a word, limiting himself to a slight tilt of the head towards Esegar, whose smug smile annoyed me.

John broke the silence by recognising the sagacity of the scholar's comment. "Brother Esegar's is an acute observation, Lord, but I would add that the Almighty helps those who help themselves."

Familiar with John's technique of not expounding on a point until pressed, thus making his argument more effective, I gazed around to see who would contest him. Unsurprisingly, it was Esegar.

"Are you saying, Brother, that the King's victory was not born of our King's unswerving obedience to God's will?"

John favoured him with the smile of a father indulging his child, and said, "Brother Esegar, our triumph today was the fruit of the superiority endowed by the use of our horses. This affirmation must take into account that our King suggested the tactic. We should inquire of our sovereign whether his intuition was inspired by the Holy Spirit or of his conception."

Alfred turned a severe eye on my friend, causing me to worry unnecessarily.

"What then, Brother John? Do you say that more is needed than royal obedience to the divine will for victory and prosperity?" asked the King. "This is an argument that concerns me greatly as we are at our lowest ebb."

John did not hesitate because, like a good chess player, he was several moves ahead.

"Indeed, we must cherish *wisdom* to ensure the wellbeing of the nation. God is swift to reward the wise: hence my earlier statement. With your permission, Sire, I would go on to propose a plan to save Wessex from its enemies."

"I am listening." The King's piercing eyes caught in the candlelight and, for a moment, seemed to flash.

John raised his beaker and took a swig of ale, aware of the faces around him scrutinising his face eagerly. Then, he spoke. "Sire, after today, Selwood is no longer a safe retreat. The pagans will seek to avenge their comrades, so we must change our strategy. I have heard tell of marshland to the west. If we could find an island there approached by just one causeway, we could defend it against anyone. But I do not propose merely passive resistance."

"What, you mean to have us skulk in the wetlands to die of the marsh fever? The idea is absurd!" Esegar cried.

Casually, John lifted his beaker, downing the rest of his ale then ending with a satisfied smack of his lips. "I have not finished, Brother," he said with the confidence of one who knows his mind. "Just as King David was constrained into the wilderness and survived by his wits to reign over Israel, so too will our King send a message of hope to his people, giving them a time and place to gather in force."

Esegar made to speak, but a royal hand gestured to silence him.

"Brother John, I know of such an islet in the marshes. It can be reached by but one causeway. So, we have our place; we shall need to establish another more suitable for the Saxons to assemble in strength. And what of a date?"

"Sire, I suggest some seven weeks after Easter, for the weather at the beginning of May will be fine for mustering."

"I object!"

All heads turned towards Brother Esegar, mine included.

"First of all, David hid alone in the desert, changing his hideaways continually to evade King Saul. How does our learned friend imagine we can hide the fyrds of three shires?"

"I do not propose hiding them—I suggest concealing the word of their mustering. Every Saxon leader will be admonished not to reveal the time and place of the assembly. Everyone will march to the same place at the same time. Once there, the host will be great enough to defend itself from Guthrum and his horde of savages."

King Alfred raised his drinking horn, his voice heavy with emotion. "A toast my friends! To *wisdom* and the wise Brother John!" I still wonder if I was the only one at the high table who noticed that Esegar failed to join in.

King Alfred was too preoccupied to observe anything. He was busy making plans for the morrow when he would convene our other two bands to head westwards to the retreat in the marshes known, at that moment, only to Alfred. Mentally, he was formulating a list of ealdormen and thegns to contact for the muster at Easter. I dare say that he intended, even as early as that evening, to draw on the fyrds of Wiltshire, Hampshire, and Somerset—for that was what happened in reality. First, however, I will relate the tale of how we arrived at Athelney.

Having gathered all our forces in the eastern stretches of Selwood Forest, we proceeded cautiously until the King called our first halt in a place of chalk uplands and valleys where I noticed a river flowing in the valley.

"It is the Stour, Brother Gwyn," said King Alfred, following my gaze. "See, over yonder"—he turned in the saddle to address John—"that large stone, standing alone, is named Egbert's Stone, because on that spot my ancestor held his court. Here, three roads meet at a point where Wiltshire, Somerset, and Dorset come together. Do you not think, Brother, that this could be the rallying place in May?"

"Is it well known to the men of those shires?" asked my friend, scrutinising the dolmen.

"It is."

"Let it be your choice, then, Sire."

Leaving Selwood behind, we dropped down towards the Somerset levels where, in an overnight encampment, the King told us about our destination. "We are headed for a place known as Aetheling's Isle: where the saintly hermit Aethelwine, son of Cynegils, King of the West Saxons, retreated.

What finer location for another member of the royal lineage to make his base?"

Thus, Alfred revealed the royal connection, but the next day we saw why there was no better place. We moved on at dawn, but for the next two hours the land was shrouded in low-lying mist. The day was fine, so I could imagine that on a day of low cloud and wet weather, the land would be invisible to a foe. The King ordered a native of the marshlands to serve as a guide. He proved essential as the whole area was boggy marsh and floodwater with a few low-level islands. Through these watery marshes along hidden pathways, thick with reeds and withies, we would have been lost but for the local knowledge of our guide.

At one point, we came to a track where the scout addressed the King, "Sire, we call this the Cut Road. Not far now to the causeway at Lyng."

When we reached the spot, John's grasp of military matters urged him to say, "Here, Sire, we should dig ditches to protect against access." We picked our way along the causeway, aware of the treacherous ground to either side. As we approached the isle, I understood what a perfect choice the King had made. Ahead were two small summits divided by a shallow depression. We gained the western summit where the King intended to build a fortification. The mist had cleared so that John was able to survey the surrounding land. He took the guide by the arm and pointed to the northeast.

"Yonder hill, is it accessible?"

"Ay, Brother, yon's Barrow Mump. I know how to reach it."

"Good, we shall need it for an advance defence. From there, our men can signal approaching danger."

His gaze swept around and settled on another hill to the southeast. Following his stare, the guide murmured, "Aller Hill …"

I understood John's thinking. Any high ground in this watery wilderness would have strategic importance for the defence of the Aetheling's Island, which local folk called Athelney. We remained there for seven weeks, occasionally sallying forth to harass groups of raiders in the area, never failing to leave them as corpses for scavengers to tear at the flesh. The rest of our time was devoted to building and digging fortifications whilst others built a forge and concentrated on transforming into weapons the iron ore brought laboriously from the Brendon Hills, distant three leagues.

One day, tired of working on the defences, I accompanied the miners. Our men dug in an ancient bell pit, which still supplied the ore we sought. I took my turn with the pick and experienced the thrill of striking an iron lode. When scops sing of our King's triumph, they say nothing about the calloused hands that underlay and contributed to our great victory.

ELEVEN

EGBERT'S STONE, MAY, 878 AD

The seven weeks between settling at Athelney and the mustering date saw an intensive message campaign, with messengers travelling as far afield as Hamwic and back. The response to Alfred's well-couched appeal was encouraging, although it remained to be seen how many thegns would honour their word. King Alfred did not allow the Danes to approach anywhere near our causeway. Well-prepared scouts informed us of their every move. Most Viking sorties aimed to gather food for the pagan army occupying the captured royal vill of Chippenham. Those straying too far south inevitably did not return as we intercepted and slaughtered them. The King's reputation as an arch-enemy of the Norsemen, confined mostly to Wiltshire and Somerset, grew proportionately. With hindsight, I feel that the success of these forays helped swell the numbers assembled in May.

The appointed day arrived, with the roseate dawn light sculpting our anxious faces. Almost two months of messaging would now be put to the test.

"Summon the men!" Alfred's curtness revealed his anxiety. In this mood, we rode along the causeway, knowing that we were leaving our haven perhaps forever. The time had come to confront the whole Great Heathen Army.

"May God be with us, Brother John," I said, drawing my horse next to his.

"We shall see if His countenance shines forth upon us at Egbert's Stone," replied my practical friend. His reply did not ease the worry in my breast. We entered the Forest of Selwood, as far as we could tell, unobserved. I swear the ride under the canopy of fresh leaves was the longest of my life as my mind dwelt on all the permutations. Would the fyrds be there? Would we have enough men to challenge Guthrum? If not, what ought we to do? And so forth.

John's thoughtful silence hardly helped my state. Was he as anxious as I? Who could tell? At my advanced age, I now realise the most futile emotion in life is worry. It does no good, for it cannot change fate; it only erodes confidence and good cheer uselessly.

About two leagues before Egbert's Stone, we spotted movement ahead. King Alfred, fearing a Danish spy, was about to send men to capture him when the fellow broke into a run towards us. Alfred stilled his tongue and reined in his horse. The man, with a bow and quiver full of arrows slung across his back, knelt before his King.

"Sire, good to see you!"

That was all he had to say until Alfred dismounted, raised him to his feet and commanded, "Fellow, whence do you come? Are you alone?" He gazed over the man's shoulder into the woods.

"Sire, I am one of the men of Hamwic." He turned and pointed along the track. "The shire fyrd is gathered at a great stone, awaiting your arrival, Lord. There are men from other shires, too," he said eagerly. "Ealdorman Aethelhelm stationed me here as a lookout against Norsemen, Sire. I am alone."

Alfred smiled, showing his approval. After ascertaining the scout's name, he said,

"Frowin, you will stay at your post until I send for you. If you see Danes, you know what to do!"

I confess, the lookout's words heartened me, and judging by Alfred's smile and John's aside to the King, I was not the only one with raised spirits.

"This is good news, Sire," I heard John say. "It sounds like there are vast numbers at the Stone. They cannot stay assembled in the forest. The trees serve to cloak an enemy."

"What, then?"

"Find a local man, Lord. There must be an easily defended place hereabouts. Seek it out, then leave a few men at Egbert's Stone to alert the latecomers to our whereabouts."

"As ever, sound counsel, Brother John. You will find me a generous lord," he added mysteriously.

When we arrived at the designated place, the greatest men of three shires were standing next to the dolmen awaiting their King. After the warm greetings and embraces, Alfred singled out an ealdorman.

"Ealdorman Hartbert, I believe your estates lie hereabouts—"

"Ay, Sire." The nobleman's anxious eyes scrutinised his monarch's face. His lands, like those of many, had suffered depletion. He could not feed this great host. His taut facial muscles relaxed as the King explained himself.

"I seek a place nearby with commanding views, easily defensible."

"Cley Hill, Lord. O'er yonder," he said, pointing vaguely.

"Ealdorman, you will lead this army to the summit. There,

we will wait overnight. By morning, all the latecomers will be here. Then we will be prepared to attack the Danes."

"The men of Somerset are ready, Lord," he replied with heartening certainty.

\My spirits rose as I watched the Somerset fyrd follow the ealdorman. The fyrd of that shire alone was a formidable force without reckoning the men of Wiltshire and Hampshire, who followed after them. We waited patiently beside our King, who broke our pensiveness.

"Brother John, your counsel has proven itself invaluable. We have enough men to sweep the Norsemen out of Wessex."

In truth, there wouldn't have been a single Saxon heart that doubted the veracity of his statement, but only a chosen few heard it at Egbert's Stone. Had we known all the facts as we smiled grimly in the forest, our certainty would have been greater: none of us knew about the divisions among the Vikings. Later, we discovered that the chieftains Uffa and Ivar had quarrelled with Guthrum, withdrawing their men. We were aware of the great storm of the previous year that wrecked 120 longships off Swanage, drowning many crews. Among the Saxons, that disaster was accepted gratefully as an act of Providence, but it had not prevented the Vikings subsequently sweeping all before them. The balance had tipped in our favour with the muster at Egbert's Stone. Our bravado was not misplaced, but words are only so much air. Nonetheless, the sheer numbers that had rallied to Alfred diffused courage throughout our host. When we joined them on the hill, I could see it reflected in every man's determined eyes. Alfred recalled the lookouts: they were not necessary, given the vantage point that Hartbert had chosen. Any movement below, other than in the forest, was easily discernible.

I would say that on the eve of the great battle John slept like a babe, except it's impossible to hear an infant snore so loudly.

With a huge sigh, I lay my ear in the crook of my arm, flung the other over my head and, despite my annoyance, finally lapsed into the sleep my body craved. Like the last leaf to fall from the tree, I rose to find the whole army preparing for battle. That is my sharpest memory of that fateful day. The rest is a chaotic blur.

The King planned to march on the Danes enclosed in his vill of Chippenham. As it happened, the overconfident Norsemen preferred to set out to meet us. The two armies came face to face at Ethandun, not far from Chippenham. The terrain gave neither side an advantage, so John and I dismounted to join the shield-wall. During my long lifetime, there have been many battles before and since Ethandun, but none has seen the equal of that dense shield-wall.

The Saxons held firm against a mighty foe. Such was the force of our warriors that after hours of hacking and hewing, they overwhelmed the Vikings and pursued them and smote their backs, leaving a trail of slaughter.

I hastened with John to untether our horses. Galloping in pursuit, we unlatched our axes to crash them down on fleeing Norsemen. One after another, we slew a score of Danes each, only halting our blood frenzy at the King's command. Before I go on, let me say, unknown to us, we had just won one of the most decisive battles ever fought in Angle-land.

Only at the King's intervention did we see the walls of Chippenham and Viking archers on the ramparts waiting for us to gallop within range to pick us off.

"Hold!" cried Alfred, galloping up to John and seizing his reins so forcibly that his steed reared in protest as the cruel steel bit on its tongue. If Alfred had done that to me, I'd not have remained in the saddle, as John managed, but might have broken my back on the hard ground. Luckily, my mount was some paces behind John's whence I saw everything, including the enraged scowl at his sovereign. Neither of us had realised the meaning of his action until he pointed at the menacing bowmen.

"Do you wish to be a modern-day Sebastian, Brother John?"

Only then did my friend's devilish glare flee from his face, replaced with a grin of gratitude.

"Only if it meant finding my Irene, Sire," he jested irreverently.

It says much of our King's preparation in theology that he understood this risky witticism. I confess, it baffled me at that moment on the battlefield. I ascribe my confusion to my reeling senses and fatigue. I asked John about it later, who scolded me.

"Come, come, Brother Donkey, surely you know that Saint Irene of Rome rescued and healed Sebastian of his arrow wounds."

"I thought he died a martyr."

"So, he did. Shortly after his recovery, he hied off to Emperor Diocletian to warn him about the consequences of his sins. As a result, they clubbed him to death."

To this day, I'm convinced that King Alfred saved our lives under the walls of Chippenham. The defeated Vikings who succeeded in entering the fortress were destined to go hungry. King Alfred besieged his royal vill, giving instructions to remove all food in the neighbourhood so that any likely Danish sortie for provisions would fail. His plan to starve them into surrender was successful. Two weeks later, Guthrum sued for peace.

In the King's tent, we discussed the terms he should impose. King Alfred had two fixed ideas: the Danes would have to supply hostages so that he could be sure they would not invade Wessex again; secondly, he wished to redraw boundaries, especially with Mercia in mind. By taking the territory previously known as the Kingdom of Hwicca, he would make Wessex more secure on its north-western boundary. To achieve this, surrounded by his available counsellors, he mooted the idea of conceding an area of England where the Danes would be free to impose their customary laws. Principally, this would cover territories north of the Humber and east of the Trent. On the whole, the Wessex lords were satisfied with these ideas. The King would propose them to the Norsemen shortly.

The most controversial suggestion came from my friend John.

"Sire, why not insist with the Danish king that he should embrace baptism? If you were to make it a condition of peace, he would be forced to accept it, given his weakened circumstances."

This idea was met with stony silence until Brother Esegar, who had been looking at one ealdorman after another in the desperate hope that they would quash the motion, finally intervened. "What sense has this proposal, Sire? To insist that a heathen adopt Christianity is to court disaster. The Holy Spirit should move a person to assume our faith. We should not force him at sword point."

"How do you reply to that, Brother John?" King Alfred asked mildly.

"Lord, we must not forget that our ancestors were pagans. Did not the missionary Winfrid cut down the oak sacred to Thor? Thus, began the Christianisation of my Germanic forebears. Can Brother Esegar assert with absolute certainty that the idea to baptise Guthrum did not come to me thanks to the Holy Spirit?"

He threw down this speculative gauntlet, but Esegar did not pick it up. He merely shrugged and muttered, "This will not end well."

He was wrong, because when Alfred met with Guthrum at

Wedmore, the chieftain agreed a treaty stipulating his conversion; they agreed on the Danelaw and Guthrum provided hostages, swearing that he would never invade Wessex. Later, this verbal agreement was ratified in written form. King Alfred, with exquisite irony, appointed Brother Esegar to instruct and prepare the Danish leader for baptism. He drew the resentful priest apart and told him to stress the ethics of Christianity in the hope that the Viking would respect the treaty. The monk reserved his most venomous glare for John, who pretended he hadn't noticed. The King ended by addressing the same words to Esegar that he had uttered to my friend in the forest: "You will find me a generous lord, Brother."

Esegar must have performed his task well, because Guthrum willingly came with thirty followers to undertake baptism at Aller, near Athelney, in Somerset. The Dane took the baptismal name of Aethelstan accorded to him by Alfred, who was his sponsor, and adopted him as a son. After twelve days of celebrations, Guthrum withdrew his army from Chippenham, taking it to Cirencester in Mercia where they remained for a year before King Aethelstan withdrew into East Anglia. In that kingdom, on the whole, he ruled wisely and well, justifying the decision to baptise him. Guthrum was no longer considered a threat to Wessex.

That was not to say that the Viking menace was over. King Alfred was too intelligent to imagine that. So, he appointed John as his military adviser; this appointment proved to be another of the King's most acute moves.

TWELVE

Countisbury, North Devon, late spring, 878 AD and *the Thames Valley, 878-9 AD*

"Sire, I have ridden through the night to bring this news."

The messenger gasped out his warning whilst swaying from exhaustion, his eyelids drooping involuntarily. "We saw a fire signal blazing just before dusk. After I left Cynwit, my journey took me to a clifftop where I saw three beacons flaring along the coast towards the open sea."

"Which means," said King Alfred to John, "they have sighted a Viking fleet in the Channel. You are my military adviser, so take a horse to Cynwit and organise the defences." Alfred replaced the messenger, too exhausted to ride out urgently as the situation demanded, with a guide. I still wonder why John insisted on my presence unless it was for my prowess with a battle axe. Anyway, the three of us galloped out along the causeway just as the sun rose to turn the land into a dazzling water world. We veered onto the coastal route westwards and saw the Viking fleet below us heading in the opposite direction.

How appropriate our destination was—a place called Wind Hill—because we rode as fast as if driven by a gale. I don't remember ever having urged a horse before to its physical limits. The foam at its mouth and its trembling body, emanating steam on our arrival, haunts me to this day. Arriving before the Vikings made the poor beasts' sacrifices worthwhile. John presented himself as King Alfred's adviser on military matters to the sceptical Ealdorman Oddo, the greatest man in North Devon.

"I know nothing of such a counsellor, but you are here; two heads may well be better than one," he conceded.

Not that there was much to think about. There were two stark choices as John pointed out: defend or attack. Messengers alerted us to the Vikings, led by Ubba, with twenty-three ships bearing twelve hundred men landing at Combwich, close to where we had seen them. Their eleven leagues to the east gave us time to ready the men with weapons and devise a strategy.

"The Norsemen will learn that the thegns have sought refuge here," John offered. "So, reduce the number of men on the rampart walkways."

"What!" The ealdorman's outraged expression revealed his perplexity.

"That way, they will underrate our strength. They will besiege us, relying on us to surrender owing to lack of water. As I said before, either we defend or attack. Let them encamp overnight and, before the dawn, we will surge out of the gates and overwhelm them."

The old campaigner grinned at John. "I see why our King sent you: it might work!" He added thoughtfully, "The men will have to rise early, respecting total silence." He gathered his thegns and explained our plan. As usual, John snored through the night. But, to his credit, he woke and dressed before the dawn. He smiled his approval as he saw my whetstone lying on my bed, since I had already honed my axe blade.

Outside in the courtyard, an unnatural quiet charged with tension greeted us. Ealdorman Odda nodded and, with a gesture of his right hand, indicated the men. Each took his vow of silence to heart. Slowly, the gates swung open on hinges well-oiled for the occasion. We poured out towards the enemy camp. Selected archers picked off a lookout with a horn to his lips to blast out an alarum that never came. A volley of blazing arrows pierced the canvas tents and set them alight. The slumbering foe emerged enraged and sleepy-eyed, poorly dressed to defend our aggressive onslaught from which they never recovered. With John, I ran towards the *Hrefn*, the raven banner of the Viking chief. Uffa, the son of Ragnar Lodbrok, one of the most-feared Norsemen of the day, met Odda's charge shield to juddering shield. They fought long and hard whilst John and I dealt with his closest defenders. I cannot describe the handplay between the two leaders—I was hard-pressed by a tall Viking with filed teeth. I remember that detail, and that he had not had time to tie back his long, blond hair. It hampered him now in the fighting as he was forever tossing back his head. On one of these occasions, I seized the opportunity it afforded to strike so swiftly and accurately that my razor-edged blade sliced the great vein in his neck, sending blood spraying to spurt his life away.

The advantage of our surprise attack cannot be understated. I believe that Odda slew Uffa thanks to his superior armour. The Viking leader was fighting with only a leather jerkin to protect his chest, against a fierce Saxon wearing a mail shirt. Even as I sought in vain for another adversary, I saw Odda transfix the Norseman's body with his sword. The leather could not resist the honed blade driven with the full force of a lunge.

The battle was ours. When we raised the raven banner with our victorious cries resounding in our ears, we could not imagine the importance of the triumph.

With the hindsight provided by the event-packed decades since then, this ancient chronicler can state with confidence that it served two purposes. First, it proved that not only King Alfred among the West Saxons was capable of defeating the Vikings, which was inspirational for their morale. Second, John had shown the importance of well-defended burhs and, above all, how to take the best advantage of them. This information he carried back to King Alfred, along with the *Hrefn*.

Two Viking armies menaced Wessex when a large fleet arrived and stationed itself at Fulham on the Thames. It threw into sharp relief Alfred's wisdom in sending his military adviser to face the Viking threat at Cynwit. We all realised that the first Viking menace after the decisive Battle of Ethandun would not be the last. I would say that the period between the autumn of 878 and the summer of 879 was the most anxious time for the West Saxons with this storm cloud ever looming.

The King summoned John to him, who as usual took me along on account of my prodigious memory. Alas, how I wish I could still draw upon its prodigies! The King stood in front of a large chart of southern Angle-land. He jabbed his forefinger at Cirencester.

"Here is Guthrum, whom we have the pleasure of knowing well," the monarch said with a grim smile. "Many Danes have gone to join him since our victory no doubt attracted to his fame as a warrior and generous lord." Without further comment, his hand moved in an arc towards London, where it hovered before settling on Fulham. "Here, we have a very large fleet of Norsemen arrived from their homeland. My spies inform me that these Vikings have contacted the Viking army farther upstream, north of the river." The King looked up at John with an expression of loathing in his eyes. "You can see what this means for my Kingdom, Brother John."

"Ay, Sire. Situated thus, they prevent our access along or across the Thames. Not only that"—he moved closer, his fore-finger tracing a line over the map—"but they command the Akeman Street with its crossing over the Thames at Staines. They have a dagger pointed at the heart of Wessex, whilst also controlling the wealth of London."

Alfred straightened, crossed his arms over his chest and sighed.

"If Guthrum breaks his oath and joins with them, we are in deep trouble, John. What do you suggest?"

As ever, John's mind had been racing as he contemplated the map. The twin threat had a galvanising effect on him, but more importantly, also on his sovereign. Once more, John's finger hovered over the chart before he took it away to scratch his head, pondering what strategy to adopt. When it came to him, he was succinct.

"Lord, we must construct a system of fortresses in Wessex and central Mercia. Then, you should assume overlordship of Mercia."

King Alfred, like everyone else debating with John, did not wait before challenging his provocative statement. "I hardly think that King Ceolwulf will accept my overlordship. Also, how do you suppose we can build a system of fortresses in the short time we have at our disposal?"

John, ready as usual, dealt with the second question. "You will have to command your lords to provide one man for every hide of land in the areas we require a fortress. I calculate that we have fifteen months to complete them, because they will not talk Guthrum into attacking Wessex before this winter. We have his hostages and he is still smarting from defeat."

He paused to let this affirmation register. Since Alfred did not object, he continued.

"A team of four men can dig out and pile up a seven cubic foot length of a defensive wall in a day." He frowned in concentration. "So, let's say a wall of 2280 yards, with a width of 20 feet and a height of eight feet, working five days a week ... the entire perimeter should be completed in fourteen weeks, Sire. There would need to be a paved walkway of laid stones on the turf and timber revetments on top of the bank. So, let's double the time needed, which becomes eight months from start to finish."

Alfred looked impressed and more cheerful. Under his breath, he murmured, "It can be done!"

A weak objection followed. "The paving stone would need to be brought from a quarry—"

"Quarrying can begin tomorrow," John said, swatting it aside. His tone changed to one of practicality again. "We must allow for bad weather, human error and the like, so realistically we'll need twelve of those fifteen months rather than eight. But it can still be done. What say you, Sire?"

King Alfred clapped him on the back. "You showed the value of a garrison at Cynwit, my friend. But where shall we construct our defences?"

Again, John was ready for this. His finger returned to the map. "We'll need other constructions meanwhile, such as bridges, causeways, streets, gateways and watchtowers." He said the last word with a flourish followed by a grin. "All the fortresses will be functioning by next summer." The hand moved slowly along the northern border of Wessex from east to west. It settled on Bath. "A fortress here would serve two purposes: it commands the Fosse Way"—he stabbed a finger down on the chart—"leading from *Cirencester*. Secondly, it blocks access up the Avon to Viking ships. They control the Channel at the moment."

The King nodded enthusiastically. "Agreed. We shall erect a fortress at Bath. But what about here?" The monarch showed he was no slouch in military matters when his finger settled on Malmesbury. "Here on the hilltop, we shall build another, as the place commands the border and the Fosse Way again."

John's face registered his pleasure, for the King not only understood his plan but was a willing participant. My friend pointed to Cricklade. "Here is a crossing of the Thames by the Ermine Street—and talking about the Romans, Sire, who were experts in military matters, we can restore some of their old fortresses, but that is by the way—which leads from Gloucester directly into Wessex."

"Mmm ..." Alfred followed intently and with understanding. "With these three strongholds, we will have blocked the main routes of Viking access and also the sea route: very good."

"We must turn our attention to the army at Fulham."

In a whirl of gestures, John indicated Wallingford, Sashes and Easting: three strategic places that, as he pointed out to his attentive monarch, would secure the entry points to eastern and central Wessex. The island site of Sashes controlled the Thames crossing by the Roman road from St Albans and the Watling Street to Silchester, as well as passage up the Thames. Wallingford was near where the Icknield Way crossed the Thames from the north-east and Watling Street, leading into central Wessex.

"By building bridges at Wallingford and Sashes, Sire, we can defend the upper reaches of the Thames from longships."

King Alfred, who was a great admirer of anything Frankish, could not resist. "I see you are thinking along the lines of the Franks, John."

"Certainly, Sire. I lived in Frankia and observed the countermeasures employed against the raiders."

"You learnt your lessons well, to our benefit."

John smiled and finished off his plan with Eashing, blocking navigation up the River Wey, the Thames tributary offered another route into Wessex. The King congratulated John on his military astuteness and, he, basking in a glow of satisfaction added, "It's more a deterrent than anything, Sire, for the Danes know that if they attempt to take one of these strongholds, their losses will be heavy at the gates. Hence, they will be reluctant to attack. On the other hand, maintaining an armed garrison means we are ready to react if they raid in the surrounding territory."

With this, both the King and I, a passive listener, thought he had finished. Not a bit of it. John had not yet come to his masterstroke—Southwark.

"We should take the initiative away from the Vikings at Fulham, Lord. If we build a double fortress with a bridge here at Southwark and restore London Bridge, we will truly menace them."

Taking the initiative appealed to our sovereign, within a week orders went out around the kingdom and construction began on every chosen site. The crucial double-fortress at Southwark, like the others, was finished by the summer of the following year just as John had predicted. With London Bridge, it challenged the Vikings on the north bank of the Thames and those at Fulham, curtailing their freedom of movement along the arterial river.

More than a year had passed since our arrival in Alfred's court, and neither of us had been allowed the time to exercise those skills for which we had been summoned. That is not to say that we sat around doing nothing—far from it. I followed John like a faithful hound as he travelled around Wessex inspecting and supervising the fortresses under construction. Also, he undertook restoration projects at places he and Alfred had not discussed on that first day. He organised a massive new ditch around the Roman walls at Winchester, doubled in width on the western approaches. Whilst there, he had the ancient stone blocks refurbished. Exeter underwent similar treatment as did Wareham.

In all of this, John enjoyed Alfred's unwavering support, because he wished to emulate Frankish culture while the significance of Rome to his family played its part. Finally, Alfred desired to concentrate centralised functions in a small number of sites to aid the protection and exploitation of trade.

I have related this plan at length because, as I will reveal later, it marked a turning point in our lives, but also in that of King Alfred's.

THIRTEEN

ATHELNEY, SUMMER AND AUTUMN, 879 AD

"What do you think of my choice of a sanctuary, Brother John?" said King Alfred, peering through an early morning mist along the causeway, where the second or first fortress—according to one's point of view—lay shrouded and invisible. Construction of the raised track had required considerable labour; either side stretched a watery wilderness only crossable by punt. Nobody could dispute that the site formed a redoubtable defensive enclave. John's military knowledge had led him to advise further building of the double-burgh model. On that morning, my friend probably asked himself like I had why the King should formulate such a question. He always had a reason, yet a monarch's query, however banal, must be answered.

"As a choice, I think it would be hard to surpass, Sire."

"Ay, that was also my thought, Abbot John."

I'm still not sure who was more shocked of the two of us at that moment. Alfred was too lucid for his manner of address for this to have been a lapse.

Since John remained speechless, the King laughed and, placing a hand lightly on his shoulder, reminding him,

"Did I not say that you would find me a generous king? Well, Abbot, I intend to build your Abbey here at Athelney. You have all of the qualities to make a splendid Father Superior." He grinned and turned to me. "Let me guess who will be your *amarius* and make of Athelney the leading scriptorium of the realm."

I can't remember whether John knelt to kiss the King's bejewelled hand out of gratitude, but I know I did. It little mattered that the Abbey had still to be built, just knowing that it would rise in an easily defended position filled my heart with joy.

I would have been even happier had I known what was about to happen. One of the King's scouts arrived later in the day, from London, with uplifting news.

"Sire!" The warrior could not refrain from beaming. "The Viking fleet at Fulham has sailed!"

"What! How can that be? Have they overwhelmed our forces at London Bridge?"

I exchanged glances with John. Unlike the King, we had understood the messenger's mood to be jubilant. How could that be if Viking ships were bearing down on Wessex?

The fellow's grin grew wider. "Nay, Sire, on the contrary! The Norsemen have left for the Continent."

"Are you sure?" The disbelieving monarch stared intently at the scout.

As the bearer of good news, he met the piercing blue eyes with an unwavering gaze. "Lord, my informants heard the Norsemen talking about *easier pickings* on the Continent. We even know that they are sailing for Ghent."

"By God, are they?" Alfred looked thoughtful. "They seek to profit from the Franks' succession dispute. Also, our defences have dissuaded them from attacking us, John. They would have lost many men attempting to breach them. We have found the best way to defend the realm."

John grunted non-committedly.

"What is it? Are you not as joyful as we are?"

John shook his head. "There is still Guthrum in Cirencester and an army north of the Thames. We must not lower our guard."

"We will not. It comforts me that we have Guthrum's hostages."

"We do, but the Norsemen set little store on life and are known oath-breakers."

This pessimism was ill-founded for, in the mid-summer, further reports arrived that Guthrum had upped and left Cirencester, leaving us momentarily dumbstruck: our spies in Mercia explained.

"They tell me," said the King, using Guthrum's baptismal name, "that King Aethelstan is afraid the Vikings to the north of the Thames might seize control of Essex. To avoid this possibility, he has marched into East Anglia where his loyal followers will receive portions of land from him. There is much enthusiasm for this among his men."

"Quite rightly," replied John, "because it is good, fertile earth."

"So, everything is fine, as long as they keep to our pact. We have established the wergild for every rank of Danish society, also for ours, so no man can be injured or slain with impunity."

"King Aethelstan's withdrawal gives me an idea, Sire." John's enthusiastic tone captured instant attention.

"Ay, Abbot, tell us!" The King insisted on John's title, even if he was the abbot only of grassy tufts, alder groves, a few huts and a blacksmith's forge for the moment.

"Sire, we should build two fortresses in Mercia. It would

extend your influence farther northwards and be a declaration of intent, both to the Mercians and the other English folk, and the Vikings in East Anglia and the Danelaw itself." He stepped over to the great chart where the familiar routine of the hovering hand with curved forefinger played out as he thought. "Here and here, Sire." He stabbed the map at Oxford and Buckingham. The latter dominated the upper reaches of the Ouse valley.

"Ah, the town of Saint Rumbold," declared Alfred, vaunting his knowledge of Christian hagiolatry. He referred to a saint from two hundred years before. "I will send my son, Edward, to oversee their construction. Would this not be ideal for a double-burgh, John?"

"Indeed, it would, Sire." He did not disguise the admiration in his voice for the King's keen mind.

I know that King Edward the Elder hasn't completed building there as I dictate this account. I guess it will not be long and anyway, it is a formidable deterrent as it stands. Instead, at Oxford, John chose the natural protection of a stream flowing into the Thames, known to the locals as The Mill Stream, diverting it to produce a wide moat. As I dictate this, Oxford prospers whilst the stone watchtowers to the north and west of the town have been incorporated into churches. As John had foreseen, the effect of this decision was to bring important Mercians to swear fealty to Alfred. In the following years, he shared control of London with the Mercian King Aethelred, solidifying this alliance by marrying his daughter Aethelflaed to the King of Mercia.

Alfred's authority and power gained impetus by minting coins.

Ah, I have one here on my desk!

It is a silver peningas—what some call a *penny* or a *sceatta*. It bears the date 886 and on the front side the lettering

AEFLFR-EDRE, with the King's bust facing right. On the back is the name of the coin moneyer, a certain GRUNAL and the word MONETA. Between the two words is the Londinium monogram. I won the coin in a bet with John. Such a rarity as triumphing in a wager with my learned friend deserves a keepsake. Once more, I digress. One cannot understate the value of honest coinage to the reputation of a king. These were years when King Alfred's power and prestige became known as far afield as Rome.

Returning to my tale and the summer of 879 when the prospects of peace began to look more than a vague hope, King Alfred ordered the building of our Abbey. The monarch did nothing that fell outside his greater plan, but he did not outline this vision until he had ordered the commencement work on Athelney Abbey and transferred us, with his court, to Winchester. Since the Minster boasted a priory with scriptorium, he arranged accommodation for John, myself, Esegar, and other scholars with the prior.

Once settled there, he summoned John and me to confide his kingship philosophy and reveal the part we would play in divulging it. "I am minded, Abbot, to create a Book of Annals—it will chronicle the history of the Saxon people. I do not intend to use Latin for this and other works, as I wish to see major writings in the English language."

We considered this for a while. Unhappy that we did not greet his idea with enthusiasm, the King snapped, "Well?"John looked up, his face a picture of thoughtfulness. "English will make our task easier, Lord, but it is great and demanding work. When will it begin? Or rather, to be clearer, I mean, in what *year* will the annals start?"

The King smiled and tugged at his blond beard, considering the question. At last, he looked up and in an authoritative voice declared, "It will commence with my genealogy. The nobility of my ancestry legitimises my rule in the eyes of my subjects. We know that my line can be traced from the arrival of Cerdric and Cynric at Cerdicesora in distant 494 Anno Domini." The King clapped his hands to bring a serving girl hurrying and bowing. "Fetch wine and three of my Frankish glasses." He waited for the maid to hasten away before showing remarkable memory by reciting a list of eight names ending with, "... *Baeldaeg Wodening.*" This last name he added with a flourish, proving to his satisfaction, at least, that his family descended from Woden. "It will be in the Preface, Abbot, we shall begin the annals proper with the arrival of Julius Caesar on these shores, the departure of the Romans followed by the conquests of the House of Wessex to the present day: year by year, my friend."

"To aid us in writing a Book of Annals, which begins before the birth of Our Saviour, I fear we have little documentation."

The King waved an impatient hand. "Julius Caesar wrote the *Commentarii De Bello Gallico.* Therefore, I have acquired a copy for my scribes to draw upon. There are also the Annals and Histories of Tacitus, which are in my library. Did you know, Abbot, that there are four books to his annals? My scribes will be able to trace from the death of Augustus in 14 *Anno Domini* to 70 *Anno Domini* where they will discover the life of Agricola, to help them focus on that general's campaign in Britannia."

Once more, our King astounded us by his knowledge: all the more remarkable because it hadn't been so long since he had mastered Latin through his determination and quickness of mind.

"Other than this great project, Abbot, I intend to revive learning in my Kingdom, which has lapsed into a state of almost complete barbarism. Through books, my friends, people will learn the meaning of true kingship—the morality of rule allied to royal wisdom. That is why you, John, will select and oversee scholars to translate important works, firstly with Gregory the Great's *Cura Pastoralis*. I will dictate a preface, then you will set down the rest in English. It will be copied many times and distributed to monasteries throughout the land."

"Willingly, Lord." John did not quail at these grandiose schemes. After all, we had come to Angle-land to use our skills. Up to now, we had set them aside owing to unforeseeable circumstances in the shape of the Vikings.

"We will do the same with Orasius's *Historiarum adversum paganos libri septem*." The King smiled at John, confident that my friend knew it well. He poured to reach for the green glass vessel brimming with wine. "Also, Boethius's *De consolatione Philosophiae*," he added with a chuckle. "Of course, we can give my Book of Annals the moral stance I require. You do understand the underlying pattern of my project, Abbot John?"

"Ay, Sire, it is to educate your people in the correct nature of kingship."

"You never fail me, Abbot. Your quick mind is a gift to me from God." He raised his glass with a smile to my friend, whilst I stood there feeling inadequate. John, however, always sensitive and kind, would not leave me confounded by ignorance.

The King resumed his plans for the Kingdom. "I shall need to create an updated law code, King Ine's, for all its inherent value, is showing signs of age. I must finance a campaign of building longships, John. They will be bigger and faster than the Viking vessels since we have secured our land borders, and now we should make our coasts safe." King Alfred spoke at length about his various projects. Though my head was befuddled by generous quantities of Frankish red wine, my abiding impression was one of an able, ambitious monarch. The latter characteristic became clear when he announced his desire to establish himself as the sole ruler of a united *Angelcynn*.

There is only so much a King may confide over cups of wine, so Alfred brought the meeting to an abrupt end by saying, "The Abbey at Athelney will be dedicated to Our Blessed Saviour, St Peter, St Paul, and Saint Egelwine. It will take many years to complete. Therefore, John, my friend, we will begin on other things in the scriptorium tomorrow, when I will recite the Preface to the *Cura Pastoralis.*" He dismissed us with a wave of his bejewelled hand. I must say, I was ready to rest and take stock of this remarkable conversation and privileged insight into the royal mind. However, John would have to be my guide for a full understanding.

As the bells of the priory church chimed for Vespers, we agreed to retire after the service to the comfortable cell the King had persuaded the prior to provide for us: he was, indeed, a generous lord.

"Don't worry, Brother Gwyn; I will explain everything to you before the time comes to sleep," John promised.

FOURTEEN

*W*INCHESTER, *879 AD*

The pungent smell of a newly extinguished candle did not help my befuddlement. John's voice brought me back from the very edge of sleep. When instructing, John preferred to pose questions, which was the last thing I wanted. Even my soporific mind realised that if my session with the King were to have sense, I would need to rouse my sleepy brain and answer.

"What do you suppose the King aims to achieve by disseminating the books he mentioned, Gwyn ... Are you awake?"

"Uh, I was thinking. He seemed keen on morality and wisdom."

"So, you were following him, after all."

"Not really. You see, those books he named. They meant nothing to me."

There followed a long silence in which I heard only the wind whistling around the eaves. At last, in the profound darkness came his reply.

"The King impresses me with his astuteness: an artful choice of books. Notice how he will commence with Gregory the Great. Alfred will begin a campaign of advocacy of himself —a form of indoctrination, Brother. I'll wager that Charlemagne is his model—"

"True, the King admires everything Frankish."

John clicked his tongue, for he hated frivolous interruptions when propounding a theory. He surged on, "In his wish to cultivate the image of the ruler as a lover of wisdom and patron of learning, as well as a military leader."

"Is that why he requires you to translate the books?"

A note of exasperation came into his voice. "Brother Gwyn, stop interrupting if you seek to learn something."

"Sorry."

"As I was saying, King Alfred wants to produce a vision of legitimate, righteous Christian kingship, one that serves to protect the people from the consequences of sin by governing with wisdom. You see, Gwyn, that's why he wishes to refurbish Ine's law code, so that he will appear to his subjects to be a Solomonic dispenser of justice."

I wanted to say that I understood, but dared not interrupt.

"Are you sleeping, Gwyn?"

That was unfair. "I didn't want to interrupt," I protested.

"Good!" He could thank the dark for dissuading me from hurling my sandal at his head. As was his way, he recaptured and held my attention. "As I understand it, he will set out a programme of educational reform headed by himself and, I suppose, the bishops, to promote wisdom. Alfred believes that victory and prosperity are determined by royal obedience to the divine will. Wisdom, cherished, ensures the wellbeing of the nation. You will see, Brother, when you read the *Cura Pastoralis* that it stresses how the wise ruler must prevent the spread of sin among his subjects by setting a moral example and correcting illicit behaviour."

A conversation requires at least two participants, so I broke in with, "Do you think King Alfred can aspire to these qualities?"

"More than any prince I have encountered. If anyone can assume moral responsibility and not fall into folly, it is he."

"What about the other books he mentioned? I recall the name Orosius."

"You have a prodigious memory, my friend. That writer detailed the sack of Rome by the Goths in 410. The King has chosen it for translation because it provides a Christian interpretation of the events and how the correct exercise of power impacts a ruler's subjects. In Orosius, to give you an example, you will find the immoderate behaviour of Ninus and his incestuous wife, Semiramis, whose sinful pleasure was mirrored by the conduct of the people of Sodom and Gomorrah. Think of the punishment, Gwyn, meted out by God. It's no coincidence Orosius observes that royal authority has always been granted by God. I could continue—"

"No need!" I blurted, fearing that John would protract the dull argument till the dawn. "I see why the King wants you to translate that author, because he demonstrates that the people's moral and temporal good is dependent on royal wisdom."

"Excellent, Gwyn. You have paid attention." Often, John would talk to me as if tutoring a child.

Setting aside my resentment in favour of further illumination, I asked, "What of the other author, Boethius?"

"Ah, you remembered his name, too. Well done!"

I screwed my blanket in my fist and bit my tongue.

"Well, in those pages there is a debate between Boethius and Lady Philosophy, again, the writer is concerned with righteous rule." I heaved a sigh, which my friend ignored. "In particular, the attempts to depose the unrighteous king, Theodoric. The author meditates on the precarious nature of kings' power and underscores the downfall of proud, unrighteous kings who are surrounded by their favourites at court—"

"Like us, John," I said sleepily and yawned.

"Hardly like us, Gwyn! I think that's enough for tonight. Sleep well." Before I fell asleep, I heard him murmur, "Tarquin the Proud and Nero, for example." I wondered how long his active brain would lead him to burble about this author. Too tired to care, I surrendered to deep sleep.

I woke before John, choosing not to disturb him. Instead, I preferred to think over what I had learnt. King Alfred, I concluded, read great authors and drew examples from them to improve himself as a monarch. I could admire his strength of mind and link it to his courage. As I dozed, I decided that we had made an excellent choice in coming to his court. Truth be told, it had been John's decision; I had followed in the name of friendship, but as I lay there that morning, I concluded that I would rather be nowhere else. If the Vikings returned, I would fight to the death for this noble King.

My mood became euphoric when King Alfred personally introduced me to the provisioner in the scriptorium and lauded my work in unstinting terms. The cynic in today's old white head tells me that he likely wanted John to himself to set about the Preface of the *Cura Pastoralis*. That first morning, my more youthful head swelled with his flattering words so that I would have performed any task placed before me with joy. I plunged directly into the relatively easy assignment of illuminating a lectionary for the Minster. When I am engaged in a serious work of illustration, I become oblivious to all else. My concentrated state explains why I did not notice the nudges and whispering and curious glances directed at John and me. In any case, I could never have expected anything quite so vile as what occurred in the first week of our residence in the priory.

Obnoxious rumours began to circulate about us in those

early days. Fed by an unknown malign tongue, the situation worsened so that our cheerful mood changed to bewilderment and dismay when brothers spat on the ground, muttered oaths or crossed themselves hurriedly when we passed. At first, I gave it little importance, but the dark undertones became unbearable.

"What's going on, John?" I asked as we strolled across the courtyard.

He came to a halt, bit his lower lip, avoided my eyes and mumbled something wholly incomprehensible. I seized him by the arm and was dismayed to catch a momentary expression of anguish on his normally serene countenance. John, imperturbable by nature, now growled one word but with such feeling that I had not sensed in him since the hours before the Battle of Ethandun. *"Insinuations!"*

Perplexed, I repeated the word but with an interrogative tone. "What do you mean?" I added.

"Have you not heard the calumnying in the cloisters? The whispers in the services? Someone is defaming our characters, breaking the ninth commandment."

"Bearing false witness?" I said and gasped in dismay. Again, I clutched his sleeve, but he shook my hand off angrily— so unlike him.

"Do not give them a further opportunity for their malicious gossip, my friend."

Sometimes I can be quick on the uptake, as on that occasion. "Nay! They surely cannot believe we have a relationship *contra naturum?*"

"That is what a scandalmonger desperately seeks to imply."

My heart began to thump, fit to burst, and I learnt for the first time what a red mist before the eyes meant.

"It's a depraved lie!" I cried without caring that others would see and hear. Unfortunately, several brothers were passing at that very moment. One of them unwisely giggled and pointed at us. Not even John's powerful grip could stay my impetuous rush. I grabbed the offender by the throat and hurled him against the Minster wall with all my ferocious strength, where he crumpled in a heap to the ground. His three companions leapt on me, one's fist striking my cheek. The violence of my reaction, to my enduring shame, left two of them on the ground bleeding before John's powerful arms pinned mine to my side. He dragged me away from the scene; my incoherent rantings were less the centre of attention than the devastated group who had incurred my wrath. Not even against the Vikings had I been so frenzied and murderous. I have John to thank that my subsequent penitence was not too prolonged.

The prior summoned me with John and my bruised and lacerated accusers. He, Prior Ansleth, a distinguished-looking monk with eyes as grey as his hair, gazed sorrowfully at John and me before verifying that I, alone, was the aggressor.

"If it hadn't been for the taller one, we'd be mourning our brothers," the unmarked monk, the one I hadn't laid hands on, proffered. "He went berserk!"

"What provoked such ire, Brother Gwyn?" the prior asked. "Your hands have been admired for the fineness and delicacy of their artistic interpretations, not for brutality."

At that moment, my mind was anything but lucid, instead filled with resentment, shame and outrage. All I managed was to hang my head, downcast and speechless. Luckily, John was by my side.

"Father Prior, it is true that my friend's hand is author of magnificent images to the glory of God, but our King will testify the might of Gwyn's arm, used to effect against the Norsemen."

"Our brothers are hardly Viking foes, but they *are* Godfearing Christians," the prior said sharply.

"Christians do not spread vile gossip and false testimony against their brother monks, Father."

"We did no such thing!" protested the first speaker.

"What is it you speak of, Brother John?" the superior inquired.

In turn, John's face bore a thunderous expression, making the four monks cower. Finding the strength to name the abomination, John snarled the words rather than spoke them: "There is a foul and unfounded rumour that my old friend and I practice unnatural acts in the privacy of our shared cell. We are both prepared to swear on the Holy Book that this is a false accusation circulated and calculated to damage us."

The prior, naturally, appeared revolted but, to his credit, fixed the accusers with a piercing stare. "Do you deny that you repeated this slander? If you make false testimony, you diminish your souls."

"We only said what's on everyone's lips, Father."

"Then you deserved your beating." He turned a stern face to me. "Anger is a sin. I cannot condone the ire you allowed to transform into violence. Saint Benedict imposed restraint on his Order and you violated his principles, Brother Gwyn."

At last, my head cleared.

"I am ashamed of my reaction, Father. I repent and beg forgiveness of my brothers. I merely plead with them to ask themselves how they would feel if someone levelled such a pernicious accusation against *them*."

"Ay, they should not only ask that but also purge themselves of breaking the ninth commandment. You four will circulate among the brothers to tell them of your sin and warn them not to commit the same error, lest their prior take serious action against the venomous, wagging tongues. Beware! My clerk will check with your brothers that you have admonished them, and if he finds you wanting, you will regret it bitterly. Now be gone!"

Once the door closed behind them, Prior Ansleth turned his attention to me. He showed the qualities that had led to his appointment.

"Abbot John, my first thought was to move you into individual cells, but doing so would only aliment further these scurrilous rumours. Brother Gwyn, let this be a lesson to you. You must control your temper and pray for guidance when tested. You will hie to the confessional and learn your penance. I will intercede for you, Brother."

I mumbled my thanks, too ashamed to use my normal steady voice.

"I shall make every effort to find the instigator of this horrible slander," the prior said with steely determination.

That was when John shook me to my core.

"Father Prior, I suggest you direct your attention to Brother Esegar."

FIFTEEN

The next morning, Prior Ansleth, his face more relaxed, addressed us in a paternal fashion, explaining his meeting with Brother Esegar.

"Well, my sons, I believe we have put an end to this unwholesome gossiping. I brought Esegar here. As expected, he denied instigating the rumours, but admitted to having told some of the brothers that he had heard your voices in the depths of the night when *normal* monks are asleep."

"The hypocrite!" John pounced. "He cannot be *normal* himself if he's snooping at our door to eavesdrop at such an hour."

The prior smiled thinly. "The selfsame point I made, but he justified his nocturnal prowling by saying that he was having difficulty that night with prayer."

"Because his conscience was unclean," I contributed.

"We cannot be sure of that, Brother Gwyn," the prior reproved me. "But like a Pharisee, he cited Romans 1.27, which alone convinced me he was the instigator. He wishes to sully your names for reasons I fail to grasp."

"Envy, Father Prior," John said. "I am sure of it. Like it or not, Brother Esegar is a learned scholar, but his character is such that his desire to be in the King's good graces is so burning that it obscures the light of reason."

"Envy is a mortal sin. We must be wary of it leading him to damnation," Ansleth said. Prophetically, as it transpired. "I will rely on some of my trusted brothers to keep a close eye on Esegar's behaviour. Meanwhile, I have warned him against the sin of spreading false witness which, of course, he denies hotly. Be that as it may, he now knows that I am watching him closely."

"Thank you, Father. I'm sure we feel reassured that we will soon forget this nightmare," John said.

"When your Abbey opens its doors, you, as abbot, will have to deal with every aspect of human nature—it can be a thankless task." They chatted for a while, leaving me to ponder on Esegar's behaviour. I could not help thinking that the problem was far from solved. Unfortunately, my instinct proved correct. King Alfred had finished dictating the Preface to John, so, at least, the scholar's jealous glances and glares at my friend ceased. John returned to his desk in the body of the scriptorium to work close to me. Another thing—praise be!—that ended was the hostile manner of the brothers towards us. If anything, the forced pleasantries and smiles revealed their shame at their previous mistreatment. Even the three victims of my rage managed to affect a kindly unconcern, which made everyday life much more pleasant.

The passing days spent working on our respective books lulled me into lowering my guard. I believe that I even greeted Esegar courteously more than once.

The brothers who tended the monastery garden also looked after a small but productive orchard, which contained several apple trees. These monks were accustomed to distributing the fruit, when ripe, mid-morning twice weekly. For some reason, Esegar substituted the gardener and entered the scriptorium carrying a wicker basket of the small, juicy apples. It made a treat to break off from our toil to enjoy the dappled green and red apples. Esegar did the round of the scribes while I watched him place an apple on each desk, asking myself why a renowned scholar should be doing such a menial task. Sometimes my curiosity stands me in good stead, as on this occasion. He arrived at John's desk before mine, moving stealthily as previously, so as not to disturb the busy scribes. From under my bowed head, I saw him furtively take a red apple, larger and shinier, from his pocket and place it on John's desk. My friend did not look up from his writing, merely grunting in acknowledgement of the gift. Brother Esegar checked around slyly, but I kept my head down and pretended I'd seen nothing. Soon, he placed an apple from the basket on my desk.

"Why, thank you, Brother. A good day to you." I betrayed no emotion in my voice. When he had slipped out of the scriptorium, I swiftly exchanged my apple with John's. He was so engrossed in his translation that he failed to react as I swapped his fruit for an inferior-looking apple. I marched out of the room into the courtyard where I satisfied myself that Esegar was not in sight before sniffing tentatively at the apple, which emanated a delicious fruity aroma. Turning it in my hand to catch the sunlight, an inspection of the red peel revealed no interference. Puzzled, for a moment, I thought of taking a bite, but my suspicious mind saved me. Instead, I strolled behind the monastic buildings to the sties. Casually, without being seen, I lobbed the apple among the grunting, shuffling pigs.

When I returned to the scriptorium, John gave me an ironical smile. In a low voice, not much more than a whisper, he said, "Did you enjoy my juicy red apple, Brother?"

"Did you see who brought it?"

He had not noticed Esegar, only the apple and who had subtracted it. I explained everything rapidly.

"Thank goodness you were wide awake, Gwyn. It might have been poisoned. What did you do with it?"

"I threw it to the pigs."

"Good Lord! Do you know how long it takes to fatten a pig? All that care and attention in vain if Esegar tainted the fruit with venom."

"We'll soon know, either way."

That evening in the refectory, I overheard the name, Ohtrad, the brother swineherd. Standing and going over to the red-bearded monk who had uttered the name, I apologised for interrupting then said, "But I heard you mentioning my friend, Ohtrad. I haven't seen him recently. Is he well?"

The white teeth revealed by his grin contrasted with the fiery beard. "Oh, ay, he's right enough, which is more than you can say for his favourite hog."

Fascinated by the freckles that littered his face before disappearing into hair and whiskers, his words took a moment to register. "Why?" I asked. "What's the matter with his swine?"

"Took ill. The creature's been spewing its guts everywhere. Brother Ohtrad was beside himself with worry. That hog is like a son to him! Well, of course, you'll know that as a friend of his. It's serviced many sows in the last few years; we've never been short of piglets. That's why our swineherd betook himself to the infirmarian for a potion."

"Did he save the hog?" I asked feeling as guilty as the worst of sinners.

"Between the healer and Ohtrad's prayers, they did. But I

say that it was the hog's brute strength that saved it. Yon beast is built like an ox!"

"What made it sick?"

The freckled brow creased. "There's the mystery. Ohtrad is adamant he served up the usual swill. He swears somebody tried to poison the hog."

"Why would anyone do that? It seems far-fetched to me."

"Ay, me too. But when you consider how much Ohtrad adores that hog ... it's enough to unbalance the sanest swineherd." He guffawed, causing curious stares and comments at the other tables.

I thanked him and returned to John. "I'll tell you outside," I deflected his curiosity. Outdoors, where no one could overhear, I recounted the facts as succinctly as possible. John, always a good listener, did not interrupt. When I had finished, his expression was grave.

"I do not have the stomach or the resistance of that healthy hog. I do not doubt that I would have devoured the apple and perished as a result. Gwyn, my friend, your quick thinking saved my life."

I basked in his gratitude later. At that moment, my thoughts centred on the heinous crime Esegar had committed. "What are we to do about this, John?"

"I must inform the prior. Together, maybe we can arrive at a solution that does not require bloodshed." The expression on his face left me in no doubt that John would have been happy to transfix the miserable scholar with the sword he kept under his bed.

"We have to stop him from trying again, John. Surely, he will make another attempt."

"Poisoners are cowards, Gwyn. I will play on his spinelessness." He visited the prior alone, so I have only what he told me afterwards on which to base this part of my account.

"Ansleth agrees with me. We have to let him know that we are aware of his crime and proceed to hold a convincing threat over him. That is why the prior will summon him after Prime to explain himself. I shall be there with you at my side."

Turbulent thoughts made it difficult to sleep, especially after what John told me: "Bring your sword hidden under your habit tomorrow, and do not take everything you see to be what it seems. I have an agreement with the prior to enact a Greek tragedy."

What did he mean by that? However much I churned it over in my mind, as I lay in bed, I came to no understanding. Frustrated, I could hardly disturb John's slumber; the only solution was to sleep to hasten the arrival of the dawn.

Seated in the choir, Brother Esegar failed to hide his shock at the sight of John in rude health. Only he among the brothers might have expected, at the least, a sickly invalid. Who can tell whether the prior's homily based on the Seven Deadly Sins struck a chord with Esegar's guilty conscience? When a brother whispered that the prior wanted to see him in his quarters, I noticed how he glanced immediately in our direction. We followed him from the minster church ten paces behind. John hauled me back when he entered the building.

"The prior will want to speak with him alone first, to ascertain his guilt. We shall delay our entry for a few minutes."

When he decided the moment was right, John stepped forward to the prior's door and knocked confidently. Inside, Brother Esegar's eyes darted from one to the other. His shifty eyes made him look foxier than ever. His wiry physique was no match for either of us should it come to a struggle, but I refer only to my thoughts at that moment. Onward, to the facts:

"Why did you accuse me of something I did not do?" he lied.

John roared, "On your knees, scoundrel!"

The quaking scholar shot the prior a terrified look that became anguished when my friend drew his sword and grasped his bony shoulder with the other huge hand.

"Kneel!" the prior ordered. I grasped my sword while the wretch wailed.

"I have done nothing!" he screeched. "You must believe me." He sank to his knees.

"Brother Gwyn, sheath your sword," Ansleth commanded. "It takes but one sword to remove a man's head."

At those words, the villain leapt to his feet, screaming and pleading for mercy.

"The same mercy you showed when you stole arsenic from the dispensary, Esegar? The same when you introduced it into the apple? Kneel, or yours will be a slower death by many cuts."

He knelt, his thin face awash with tears, but he still had the effrontery to croak, "You cannot slay a man on this sacred ground without a trial."

"Brother Gwyn"—I believe the prior's eyes twinkled—"take Esegar by the ears and stretch his neck so that it is bare for a clean strike."

I grabbed the fellow by the ears, my heart thumping, for I had forgotten John's words of the previous evening. At that moment, two people in the room believed a beheading was taking place. John raised his sword to the accompaniment of a shriek from the doomed scholar. He did not strike, although he must have yearned to bring the blade down. Instead, he said, "Father Prior, should we spare the wretch if he repents?"

"Let us hear his intentions first," the prior enacted his role to perfection. At last, I remembered the *Greek tragedy* and smiled inwardly: all playacting, but Esegar was not to know it. I will refrain from repeating the wretch's supplications, suffice it to say that he revolted my stomach and that I seriously wanted to strike at him with my sword.

In the end, it was not the threat of beheading, nor John's growled warning that should there be a repetition he would show no mercy, which intimidated the coward, but the prior's next words.

"Brother Esegar, at the slightest sign that you mean ill to either of these brothers, I will hasten straight to our King and relate everything."

Given that Esegar's motivation was his longing to supersede us in King Alfred's graces, this was the gravest threat he could receive. There followed a long sermon directed at Esegar about mortal sins, ending with the threat of expulsion and, rather excessively, excommunication. The scholar slunk out of the room as if the verbal onslaught had been a physical whipping. When he had gone, we three relaxed and John and the prior laughed when I confessed, "I truly believed we were about to behead him."

With hindsight, I wish we had.

SIXTEEN

Every time I crossed paths with Esegar, he seemed to have shrunk. I know that was only an impression. Undoubtedly, our *Greek tragedy* had the desired effect. Like a snail retreating into its shell, Esegar shied from intrigue, leaving us the necessary calm for our work. One morning, some weeks after the episode in the prior's room, John took a break from his laborious translation of Pope Gregory's opus and watched my careful inking of an initial until I had laid the quill on my desk and sat back.

"That is the most intricate letter E that I've ever seen, Gwynn. How terrifying is your green-faced beast with its sharp teeth! Will it devour those eight poor souls? They look penitent, rather like Esegar under my blade."

I laughed and explained which Biblical passage the image referred to, before politely asking how his work proceeded.

"On the whole, I am faithful to Gregory's text, whilst emphasising those passages that appertain to Alfred's vision. With the Esegar nonsense, I had no time to show you our King's Preface. Remember," he said, fumbling through sheets of vellum, "these are the King's own words. They will give you an insight into his thinking." He laid a page carefully in front of me, but rather than reading it, I admired its neatness and precision. Complimenting him on this, he then replied, "Ever the artist's eye, Gwyn! Aren't you going to read it?"

He indicated a passage. "Read from here!" I quote—*but wait! Let me check my copy*—ah, yes, here it is:

> *"So completely had wisdom fallen off in England that there were very few on this side of the Humber who could understand their rituals in English, or indeed could translate a letter from Latin into English; I believe that there were not many beyond the Humber. There were so few of them that I indeed cannot think of a single one south of the Thames when I became king."*

Horrified at the implications, I blurted, "Surely our King exaggerates, John?"

"I fear not."

He slipped another sheet over the first one.

"Here is what he aims to do about the ignorance in his realm. Go ahead, read it!"

I felt privileged, but also intellectually challenged. Was I as ill-educated as those beyond the Humber? Not everyone could be as erudite as my friend John. I trace my improvement as a scholar from that day and the following words of our admirable King, referring to the *Pastoral Care*:

> *"When I had learned it, I translated it into English, just as I had understood it, and as I could most meaningfully render it. And I will send one to each bishopric in my kingdom, and in each will be an æstel worth fifty mancuses. And I command in God's name that no man may take the æstel from the book*

nor the book from the church. It is unknown how long there
may be such learned bishops as, thanks to God, are nearly
everywhere."

"When I saw Alfred's aestal, Gwyn, I at once thought of you. It is an object of great beauty and worth. To behold it is to appreciate the King's deep love of learning. Now you understand the extent of the task before us. When I finish this, I hope before the year is out, I will proceed to a translation of Orosius and at that point, I will call upon you to illustrate my work. The King is in a hurry to send the *Cura Pastoralis* throughout the land; hence, he opted for a lack of images. As soon as I have finished, scribes will copy my work—"

"Ha!" I interrupted, "Therein lies the weakness of the King's scheme. Tremulous hands, inattentive transcribers, slapdash workers ..."

"Gwyn, we will entrust the transcriptions to our best scribes. The King dictated the Preface to be explicit. He set out an educational reform programme headed by himself and his bishops where the ultimate aim is wisdom. You don't suppose he will confer transcription on such as those you disdain, do you? The King's wrath would know no bounds should he be presented with a woeful script."

"John, I think you should provide me with a copy of Orosius. My learning has lapsed. I need to refresh my Latin and challenge my intellect, lest I become like the monks and priests the King so despises. Also, I can begin to think about the images I will include to illustrate your script."

John raised the lid of his desk and, reaching inside, withdrew a leather-bound volume. Tooled into the cover, the title *Historiarum adversum paganos libri septum.* I gazed at it, admiring the ancient craftwork. Understanding the fragility of the book, laid it carefully, to John's grunt of approval, on my work surface.

"Seven books of history against the pagans," I murmured, gaining myself an inarticulate chunter for my translation—I hoped one of approbation.

Thus, we worked on in companionable silence, for the main part, until John finished his translation of the *Pastoral Care* in the spring of 880. King Alfred, delighted with his efforts, and to accelerate transcription, ordered five carefully chosen Winchester scribes to share out the pages, so each would complete a section before exchanging the sheaves. In this way, one hand would eventually transcribe the entire volume, making five volumes ready for dissemination. Again, it took the better part of a year to do this. On completion, Alfred sent the books to five important bishoprics around his realm with instructions for further transcription within the dioceses. His aim was to inform every priest in the land of the book's contents as a guide to carry out their mission, according to Gregory's canons.

The King planned to do the same with the volumes of Orosius and Boethius.

"John, you must begin at once on Orosius, but first, there are a couple of people I would like you to meet. They will recount their travels in pagan lands."

The next day, the King came into the scriptorium followed by two men wrapped in furs, each with a weather-beaten face and the gait of a sailor. It transpired that they were both traders.

"Brother John, this is Ohthere. He has lived furthest north of all of the Norwegians."

Alfred turned to the swarthy, blond-haired traveller, whose hair was tied back with a leather thong. "John is from Saxony, Ohthere: he will have a good grasp of the regions you describe.

Interpolate his knowledge into the prose of Orosius, Brother, where appropriate."

John looked intrigued, not annoyed as I might have thought. I knew he hated interference with his work. But the King, justly, had understood that the traders' experience would enhance my friend's efforts.

"This is Wulfstan, who can describe his voyage beyond Wendland as far as Estland where, he tells me, there are many fortified settlements and each with a king. Make good use of his knowledge, Brother." The King then turned on his heel and left.

I mention this meeting to reveal how thorough Alfred was, leaving no stone unturned in his attempt to transmit learning. I will now explain what John heard and was able to include in his translation of Orosius.

"Extraordinary," said John, urging Wulfstan with a smile, "Tell me about your voyage, but skip Wendland, with which I am already familiar."

"Ay, well"—the trader pulled up a stool and sat—"we kept Langeland on our port side, followed by the other Danish lands of Lolland, Falster, and Skane."

John clicked his tongue impatiently, which I understood, for even I had heard of the latter region to the south of Sweden. Thenceforward, all the names meant nothing to me, whilst John occasionally scribbled a note. He hurried the trader along past the Swedish territories, saying that he had no time to waste. Wulfstan narrowed his eyes, but obliged by mentioning a very large river called the Vistula, which John knew. But I could tell that his interest, at last, was roused.

"The Vistula flows into the Estmere, at least five leagues wide." This Estland was the area Alfred had mentioned earlier, the one with fortresses and kings. "Ay," Wulfstan continued, "It is a land of honey and fish. The kings and powerful men drink mare's milk while the poor and the slaves sup mead. There is no ale brewed among the Este, but there is plenty of mead."

We murmured our surprise, to the trader's satisfaction having captured our interest, before he told us about the strange customs associated with death and property. To my more civilised ear, the traditions of the Este seemed incredible.

"There is a custom among the Este that after a man's death, the body lies indoors with his relatives and friends for a month, sometimes two. The kings and other high-ranking men remain un-cremated at times for half a year—the wealthier they are the longer they lie in their houses."

"How gruesome!" I muttered, and shuddered.

Wulfstan shrugged, making the bearskin draped over his shoulders seem alive, and continued his account. "Throughout the time the corpse lies indoors the men drink and gamble the deceased's fortune until the day that's fixed for cremation. They divide his property after building a pyre—whatever is left of it after the drinking and gambling—into a handful of tracts. They place the largest swathe about a mile from the settlement, then the others until all the land is distributed within the mile, so that the smallest lot is closest to the place where the corpse lies."

Tempted to ask why, I remembered my deservedly bad reputation for interrupting and held my tongue.

A cogent speaker, Wulfstan at once satisfied my curiosity.

"The men with the swiftest horses in the area assemble at a chosen point about two leagues from the property. At a signal, they gallop towards it, the fastest rider reaching the first portion of land." He smiled. "That is the largest, of course, which he takes for himself. The race proceeds in this way until all the property is shared. They cede the smallest lot to the slowest of the horsemen, which is the land nearest the settlement. Do you see how it works?"

I nodded enthusiastically. John grunted, seemingly unimpressed, but he made a sensible point: "In that case, I expect good horses are extremely valuable among the Este."

"If the King made their practice law in Wessex, everyone would be an expert rider," Ohthere spoke for the first time, displaying a fine set of white teeth when he grinned.

Our narrator, eager to pick up the thread of his tale, asserted his authority by raising his voice over his companion's. "When the man's possessions have all been distributed by the horse race or drinking and gambling, they carry out the body to burn with his weapons and clothes. Whatever other belongings survive the long period of his lying in the house are put by the wayside for strangers to take."

John scratched his beard at the chin thoughtfully, then remarked, "Someone among the Este must know how to induce cold, otherwise the dead men could not lie so long without rotting."

Wulfstan, with knowledgeable air, nodded. "One of the Este tribes practises the art; indeed, if they fill a bucket of water, they can cause it to freeze over, even in the summer."

"I wonder how they perform that miracle," I said, astounded.

"Only they know the secret," the trader looked gratified at my awe.

John looked hard at Ohthere. "I presume you have traded in different lands. What can you tell us?"

The taller of the two men, Ohthere, who had remained standing throughout his companion's tale, drew up another stool. I groaned inwardly, as I am not as good a listener as John.

"I have travelled the farthest north of all Norwegians, as I told your King. I lived in the north of Norway on the Atlantic coast. The land stretches very far north beyond that point. Nobody lives there but for a few places, where a folk called the

Finnas have their camps, hunting on land in winter and, in summer, fishing in the sea."

"Were you curious to travel into the unknown?" I asked, entering into the spirit of his adventures.

"You understand me, Brother. I wished to find out how far the territory stretched to the north, or whether anyone lived beyond the unpopulated area. So, I travelled up along the coast, keeping the wilderness to starboard and the open sea on my other hand for three days. That took me to where the whale hunters go at their farthest."

"Were you not afraid to be devoured like Jonah?" I asked.

"Hush!" John glared at me whilst Ohthere ignored my remark.

"I continued north as far as I could reach in the next three days. Suddenly, the coast turned east, or the sea penetrated the land. I could not be sure. All I know is that I waited for a following wind before sailing east along the coast for four more days. Again, I had to wait for the right wind, because the shore-line turned south. I ploughed on for five more days until I came to a great river. There, I turned up into the river, since the territory on the far side of it was settled and I knew not what reception to expect."

He paused for breath and looked at each of us in turn to gauge our interest. Satisfied, he resumed.

"You see, I had not previously come across any settled district since I left home. But, the whole way, the land to starboard was uninhabited apart from fishermen, bird-catchers, and hunters—these were all Finnas. Now, I must mention the Beormas—you've heard of them?"

I had not, but said nothing, while John nodded distractedly, which was enough for the trader to press on.

"They had large settlements in their country—the Norwegians did not dare to trouble them. But the land of the

Terfinnas was completely deserted except where hunters made camp, or fishermen or bird-catchers."

He hesitated, as if unsure of whether to proceed.

"In truth, that is the end of my tale, but not of what I learnt. As I told King Alfred, the Beormas told me many stories about their country and the surrounding lands."

"You do not know how much of it is true, because you have not seen it for yourself, I suppose," said John. "But continue. I wish to hear it."

Gratified, the trader explained that the Beormas spoke almost the same language as the Finnas. So, he felt emboldened to venture that far. "Apart from exploring, I went after the walruses in search of the valuable ivory in their tusks."

Again, he paused, then with a tone of self-importance, said, "I brought some tusks to King Alfred and he was very pleased with them. Did you know that walrus hide is very good for ship-ropes? This creature is much smaller than whales; it is about seven ells long. The best whale-hunting is in my country; the biggest are fifty ells long. With six companions, I killed sixty of them in two days. What do you think of that?"

I was wearying of his tale and his boastfulness did not help. A stern look from John sufficed to make him latch onto his account again.

"Wealth among that folk is measured in wild deer. When I sailed here to Wessex, I still had six hundred unsold tame deer. They are called *reindeer*. The chieftain I met was one of the richest in that country, but he had not more than a score of cattle, twenty sheep, and the same number of pigs—what land he tilled, he ploughed with horses. The wealth of the Beormas, however, comes mostly from the tribute which the Finnas pay them."

"What tribute is that?" I earned a reproving scowl from John.

"Mainly the skins of beasts, the feathers of birds, whale-bone, and ship-ropes made from walrus hide and sealskin. Each pays according to rank. The highest has to pay fifteen marten skins, five reindeer skins, one bearskin, ten measures of feathers, and a jacket of bearskin like the one I am wearing, or otter skin and two ship-ropes. Each of these must be sixty ells long, one made from walrus hide, the other from seal."

"The Beormas must be fearsome warriors," John said. It appeared that it was all right for him to interrupt.

Ohthere looked pensive.

"I put their hardiness down to the harshness of the country and difficulty of making it productive to feed their families. The land of the Norwegians is very long and narrow. What can be used for grazing or ploughing lies along the coast, and that is sometimes rocky. Wild mountains lie to the east, above the cultivated ground. The Finnas live among those peaks."

By now I was weary of his tale, but obliged to listen as the King had commanded us to hear the traders. Ohthere was determined to explain the distribution of the pagan population, so he turned his attention to the north.

"The country of the Cwenas borders the land in the north. They occasionally raid the Norwegians across the mountains and sometimes undergo them. There are very large fresh-water lakes throughout these mountains, so the Cwenas carry their boats overland onto the lakes and from there attack the Norwegians. Their vessels are small and light."

At last, he came to the end of his discourse by referring to places near his home that we knew. Five days sailing from his home lay the trading-town called Hedeby, which is situated among Wends, Saxons and Angles, and belongs to the Danes. When he sailed there from Sciringes heal, he had Denmark to port and the open sea to starboard for three days. Then, two days before he arrived at Hedeby, he had Jutland and Sillende and many islands to starboard. The Angles lived in these districts before they came to your land." He said patronisingly, as if we didn't know.

We thanked them both for the wealth of information they had supplied, and John promised to include much of it in his translation of Orosius. I wondered how he would do that, but thought it wiser, after all my listening, not to investigate. We watched the two fur-clad traders leave the scriptorium with the rolling gait of mariners.

"There are bold men who risk their lives to make an honest living, Gwyn. We should be thankful that our stools are soundly on *terra firma*."

"I could almost taste the spume when the tall one was speaking," I contributed. "I prefer my quill to do my travelling, John. When I pronounced these words, little did I know that my poor stomach would, once more, be tested by the ocean's roll.

SEVENTEEN

WINCHESTER, SPRING, *881 AD* AND *EAST ANGLIA, 882 AD*

The winter came and went, and during that season John and I almost completed our magnificent illustrated English version of Orosius—I beg you to allow my immodesty. The King, away on the East Anglian border, faced a period of Viking menace whereas we benefited from calm at Winchester to press on with our work.

Almost two years of undisturbed labour saw us finish the *Pastoral Care* and, surely, we would have completed the *Historiarum adversum paganos libri septum* except that a messenger arrived from the King. When the warrior burst into the tranquillity of the scriptorium, his tunic covered in dust clinging to dried blood, eyes wild and hair in disarray, I feared the worst. His disregard for the silent concentration of the scribes confirmed my apprehension.

"Who among you is John the Saxon?" he bellowed.

John stood and beckoned him, placing a finger to his lips to entreat silence.

The agitated man ignored the gesture, booming, "I have an urgent message for you from the King!"

Unperturbed, John fixed him with a stare and with authoritative tone said, "Outside!" Bemused, the messenger hesitated, giving John the time to grasp his arm and growl, "Show some respect. Some fight with their arms, others with their brains." He coaxed the warrior out of the room. "What is your message?"

The newcomer, seeking to imitate the same authority shown earlier by the scribe, drew himself to his full height and said, "King Alfred commands you and your comrade to bring your weapons and accompany me at once."

John called me. Within minutes, swords at our waists, we joined the rider.

"Let's hasten to the stables," John said.

The messenger concurred, but reserved a surprise: he left his mount with the lad, saying tersely, "We travel without horses."

Bewildered, we strode after him without an idea of whither and how we were headed. In silence he led us to the river, known to the local folk as the Icene. At a wooden jetty, a man holding a rope attached to a peculiar shallow-bottomed boat awaited us. Our companion cried, "Hurry, Brothers, no time to waste! Into the boat with you." He seized a paddle from the fellow with the cord and joined us in the vessel. We sat together on the central seat while he stepped into the stern where he deftly caught the rope tossed to him and coiled it. Taking up the paddle again, he directed us into midstream with vigour.

"Faster by boat," he explained. "With the current behind us, we'll cover the nine leagues to Hamton in no time."

As we flashed past the ancient Roman walls to the east of the city, I could see that he was right. I was enjoying the new sensation, eyes no longer fixed on a sheet of parchment but absorbing the scenery of the Winnal Moors, not bothering about the purpose of our precipitous excursion. John's character, so different from mine, meant he had little patience for admiring his surroundings.

"What has happened? Your tunic tells me there has been a battle."

The warrior glanced down ruefully at his clothing—otherwise, he never took his eyes off the stream ahead. He was aware of the fluctuations in the river height along this stretch, necessitating attention and occasional use of the paddle to steer the bows into deeper water. The King would have chosen a local man, an expert in navigating the Icene. Still, he found time to relate his tale, avoiding mishap.

"Vikings," he said abruptly, then explained. "The King received reports of the sighting of an invading fleet coming from the south. So, in all haste, we left our encampment near East Anglia and marched to the coast here at Hamwic." He broke off and grunted as he steered to avoid a floating branch. "Further news reached the King that the Nordmann fleet was approaching the Isle of Wight. They made landfall at Gosport; I reckon they meant to take Portchester, but the King wasn't having that." His voice adopted a distinct note of pride, so that even I paid attention despite the distraction of Twyford. That is where, as its name suggests, there are two fords. So, our pilot had to use all his skill to steer us over the chalk bed of the stream, shallow enough for folk to cross on foot. I noticed more watermills in that place and ascribed their presence to the force of the rushing river. We shot past them as our steersman boasted, "King Alfred set us up with a shield-wall and behind us, men with missiles, himself and his guard in the third row, and riders on either flank. He knows what he's doing, does our King!"

"From your words, friend, I take it you won the battle," John said.

"Ay, although they charged us and their horsemen tried but failed to outflank us. The King had us stretched wide so that our left and right wings thrust upon the Norsemen in the centre of the battlefield. Our cavalry chased off their mounted scouts, clearing the way for a sweep around to attack from the rear. We knew then that victory was ours. Their chieftain, Aedmund, fell under our blows, followed by great slaughter."

"Did you slay them all?" I asked as we passed East Leah where there was a vast clearing in the forest.

"Depends on what you mean." With his free hand, he brushed chestnut hair from his eyes. "Thorfinn the Nordmann, their leader, fled with the remnants: some three-score men to the Isle of Wight. But our King would not let them escape. We followed them and fought again, but with numbers in our favour, indeed, we slew them all. In truth, we captured a few who will fight for us if they wish to live."

By now, John, like me, was thoroughly confused. He asked, "You won a great victory at Portchester. Why, then, did the King send for us and ask us to bring our weapons?"

The warrior shrugged and grinned, risking John's ire. "I thought it odd to fetch two scribes. What use are monks in battle—even if they own swords?"

John's scowl wiped the grin off his face. "I'll wager I've slain more Vikings than you, for all your brash words!"

Hardly crestfallen, the cocky steersman changed the subject. "See, over there—that's a sawmill. The river powers it; yon's where they cut the planks for the King's ships. Just beyond it the water becomes tidal, but as you'll see we still have the current because it's low tide at this hour. I knew that before boarding our craft," he said grandly, as if talking about one of our monarch's new longships.

I could not help but laugh at his bold, cheeky manner, which earned me a glower. He might have looked at me kindlier had he known that I would save his hide in the days to come.

Soon, we sped under a wooden bridge.

"Yon's the Mannysbrigge", the warrior informed us. "We're nigh on arrived now."

I could see that there was movement on either side of the river where huts and houses began to appear, for first came the outlying settlement of Hamton before giving way to the important trading port of Hamwic. Our steersman veered us towards the calmer water of a wooden quay on the right bank, where he called to a fellow before hurling the coiled rope upwards for him to catch to secure it around a bollard. This brought our careering progress to a welcome halt. Drifted much farther, we'd have been in the tidal estuary.

"The King's palace isn't far from the river," he told us. "That's where we're bound."

A fine edifice made of stone, with masonry neatly composed, stood bathed in the afternoon sunlight. Judging by the array of splendid windows, the two-storey building had been constructed for the perfect enjoyment of air and the southern sun.

"I'll wager," said John, whose universal knowledge embraced architecture, "that these are Roman stones most sensibly reused."

I committed the error of showing interest. "What makes you think so, Brother?"

"Take the side windows: do they not have double semi-circular-headed lights with a flat arch enclosing them? Observe the mouldings of the exterior, too, all imitated from Roman architecture."

One day, in my illustrations, I would reproduce the details

on vellum; to which purpose I memorised the forms. Regardless of my lack of interest, John vaunted his superior knowledge.

"See how the impost of the central window is composed of an astragal and cavetto with a square fillet, detached from the cavetto by an angular groove to produce a pleasing effect. Are you listening, Gwyn?"

"Eh? I was trying to memorise the shapes for future use," I replied truthfully, which seemed to appease him. Had he been informing me about the edifice in Greek, a language I know nothing of, I'd have understood about as much—that is, nothing! To have a best friend possessed of unparalleled learning had its benefits, but also provided many moments of supreme boredom. One of the greatest advantages, the privilege of frequenting King Alfred, I owed unquestionably to John.

Our guide led us inside the palace, into a large room with a gallery. A blazing fire cast a ruddy glow onto the faces of the men seated around it. The warrior-steersman bowed to the King,

"The monks, Sire!"

"Ah, John, Gwynn, welcome to Hamwic." He clapped his hands and murmured something to a servant, who reappeared with three beakers of wine for us weary travellers. The red wine, an exquisite import from Frankia, was met with my grateful and ignorant approval. I only know what I like, whereas John licked his lips and said, "An excellent Médoc, Sire."

The King beamed and turned to the assembled thegns, saying, "Learn, my friends, what depths study can give a man. One of you asked if the wine was from Frankia. It is, but Brother John knew precisely that it comes from the land of the Medullicus."

"Medullicus?" one of the baffled thegns asked, expressing my perplexity.

The King raised an eyebrow to invite John's explanation, the very thing he yearned to do. Our King was an expert in psychology.

Swift to oblige, John expounded: "Medulli, the Celtic tribe living by the Gironde estuary—they gave their name to this fine wine."

"Just many of the wines that arrive in the Hamwic store-rooms. This port supplies many of the needs of our kingdom, not least salt. You will have passed the saltworks by the Icene on your way here," the King added.

John confirmed he had seen something that I, who had gazed around more than he, had missed.

"The shame is," continued the King, "that the pirates from the North disrupt peaceful commerce." He glanced at our warrior friend for confirmation. "You will have heard of our latest conflict with the sea wolves."

"Congratulations on your victory, Sire," I spoke for the first time, emboldened by the wine.

Alfred tilted his head in acknowledgement before raising a finger to make a point.

"That is why we are here today. As you know, I have ordered the building of new longships to combat the Viking raiders. Six ships are lying at anchor in the Channel. We sail at dawn to East Anglia. My spies inform me that more pirates are preparing to descend on our eastern shores from the Meuse estuary." The name had a familiar ring to me. After a moment, I linked it to the name I knew it by: the Maas. From maps I had seen, I remembered that the inlet was opposite East Anglia. On that coast lay the wealthy trading port of Ipswich, for sure a town King Alfred would wish to remain safe, even if outside Wessex. "I intend to intercept them off the East Anglian shore. It will be a test for our mariners"—his piercing eyes roved over the thegns—"and a trial of Saxon arms. John and Gwyn, you will fight beside me; John, you will write a record of the battle and once returned to Winchester, you will hand it to my chroniclers. They, even now, should be writing an account of our victory at Portchester. Gwyn, you will slay as many Vikings as you can."

My eyes widened while the King guffawed at his jest. To my discomfiture, the thegns joined in. To alleviate my feelings, although the joke was not at my expense, if anything being a tribute to my prowess, Alfred called for more wine for everyone. I forgave him at once. Pardoning him my exposure to the insidious currents of the English Channel the next day was far harder.

Yet, a stiff following breeze worked wonders for my queasiness and delayed the inevitable. Such was the smooth progress along the Solent that I admired the sleek lines of our accompanying longships, their colourful, billowing sails, the efficiency of the crews and the beauty of our coastline. The King's gold had maintained the warrior-sailors in over a year's training, the expense repaid by their smartness in manoeuvring the vessels when called upon.

Veering around the coast of Kent, hitting contrary current, the inevitable occurred. Facedown, hanging over the gunwales, the heaving sea flashing past below me, I emptied my not too full stomach. Even my cautious, solid breakfast of bread and cheese did not save me from the seasickness. Resigned to being the butt of jokes and the role of a confirmed land lover, I mistakenly believed the worst was passed: not so.

To lay his trap, King Alfred ordered all the canvas furled, knowing that, from a distance, the sails are the first sighting. All momentum therefore ceased, leaving the vessels wallowing with the rise and fall of the waves. This motion disturbed other members of the crew. Thus, I found myself hanging over the side in company. Amazingly, the human body can recover from such trials; when I thought I could bear no more sickness, the fresh North Sea breeze restored me.

In a condition, by then, to be aware of the circumstances around me, I noticed a lookout scramble down from his position halfway up the mast. He dashed across to the King to point to the east. My eyes sought out the horizon—if only the ship would hold still! On the rise, I glimpsed small squares of colour in the distance: Viking sails. The King walked among the men, assuring himself that the grappling hooks and ropes lay adequately prepared, sparing a word of encouragement to his brave warriors. Soon, there was no doubt about the sighting: four gaudy sails were visible and approaching. King Alfred summoned a warrior to his side, ordering a horn blast, the signal to drop the sails.

As the great sheets filled and were fastened by fixing the ropes, the steersmen veered our ships towards the oncoming vessels. We had a south-westerly crosswind in our favour whilst the Vikings tacked into it. The distance between the opposing forces closed rapidly enough for me to see the enemy hoist their large round shields aboard. The heathen custom to suspend the brightly painted disks along the gunwales was both an adornment and practical. It avoided the scramble to the prow of our men to retrieve the heaped shields.

Just in time, our men raised the wooden protectors as the air hissed thick with arrows. Even so, two fell pierced by the barbs. Undeterred, King Alfred delayed the response of our archers until the distance narrowed to such that they could see the unprotected limbs of the enemy under or around the shields. Again, a horn blast signalled the release of a devastating hail of accurately aimed darts. The Vikings had not expected a similar toll. The immediate effect was to reduce the response of the missiles to be less than ruinous. The meekness of their counter enabled our crew to aim the grapples undisturbed, so we could haul our vessel to thump into the hull of the leading longship. The ropes were made good whilst our archers picked off the foes who were attempting to slice their ship free. The resulting swaying of the bound vessels made boarding hazardous, but I saw John leap across, flatten a Viking with the momentum of his jump allied to the weight of his shield, before slashing an onrushing, screaming pagan. I flew across after him in the company of several others, one of whom caught me to stop me falling at the feet of a fur-clad Viking. In time, I raised my shield to parry the full force of an axe blow aimed at my head.

My reply, learnt on the battlefield of Ethandun, was swift and lethal. The axeman's hefty strike left him off-balance, always the moment for the counterstrike under the enemy guard. My sword drove into the momentary gap between shield and body, the blade sliding up the leather jerkin to the exposed flesh of his armpit. Experience told me to drive all my weight behind my weapon as this would take the honed steel to a vital artery. My wrist twisted as I tried to keep my grip on the hilt as my victim fell like a sack of coal. Despite the searing pain in my joint, I freed my blade from his body in time to fend off another assailant. In battle, not a moment can be lost. Otherwise, death lurks on the unwary shoulder, as it did on that of one of my comrades.

Without thinking, I slashed behind the leg of a giant Viking about to deal a fatal blow to him with his axe. I cut through the rear knee ligaments so that the monster's leg gave way, sending him crashing to the feet of his nemesis, the comrade I had saved. Only then, after he had delivered his mortal strike, did I recognise him as the guide who had steered us along the river to Hamton. A grateful grin, then we were back to our desperate hand-play.

The battle ended thanks to our superior numbers and

tactics with our victory. The crews of two ships surrendered when defeat stared them in the face, whereas the other two crews fought nobly to the last man. Our prisoners secured, the dead tossed into the deep, we set sail for Wessex.

Fighting aboard a ship is far worse than combat on a battle-field, I concluded. Space is more restricted, the motion of the sea can unbalance you, and blood-soaked planks are more treacherous underfoot than a grassy field. But I survived, not resisting to seek out our erstwhile guide.

"What use are monks in battle?" I repeated his words from the Icene.

He did not halt to reply, but grabbed me in a ferocious hug. "Thank you, Brother. I judged you ill—you saved my life."

"And, so I did!" I beamed, momentarily forgetting my apprehension at the Channel currents that would torment my return voyage. King Alfred ordered the distribution of ale. *Sea-sickness be damned,* I thought, grabbing and draining my beaker to slake my well-earned thirst. Resisting the urge to drink more of the freely-given beer, I joined in the raucous singing common to all eight ships of our small fleet. How strange that my stomach survived the return to Hamton. I ascribe it to the joy coursing through my unscathed and victo-rious veins.

EIGHTEEN

ROCHESTER, 885 AD

The King's asking of John to write an account of the sea battle set a precedent. Far from taking it as a burden, John, in his usual exuberant manner, saw reporting as an opportunity to improve the work of the Winchester chroniclers.

"Frankly, I'm not impressed," he told me after consigning his report. "The annalists allowed me to browse through their earlier efforts. You know, about the first years of the kingdom. Can you guess what I discovered, Gwyn?"

I had to admit that I could not.

"Of course, it's one thing to set down the events unfolding before our eyes but completely another to write about those of hundreds of years ago. Even so"—he screwed up a comical, unconvinced face—"where they lack documents, the scribes resort to legends and folktales. Imagine that! What will future generations think?" I could tell by his expression how outraged he was; inwardly, I believed he would have done no better in the absence of documentary evidence, but I refrained from annoying him. More justifiably, he remarked, "Not to mention the bias, Gwyn. When they write about the coming of Christianity to these Isles, they fail to refer to the Celtic church at all —and not a word about the famous Synod of Whitby!"

Scowling at my lack of reaction, exasperated, he continued.

"When I hand over the next report our King commands me to consign, I shall stand over the wretch to ensure he transcribes it without omissions."

We did not have long to wait for the royal summons, for this was a period of intense Viking activity. Thanks to King Alfred's not calling on us for the naval battle of the Stour, I avoided more sea warfare, the Lord be praised. And to his retaking of London, enough time elapsed for us to finish our version of Orosius. We even made a start on Boethius's *De Consolatione Philosophiae*. My enjoyment of illustrating the Dacian author's condemnation of Ulysses when enthralled by the sorceress, Circe, was interrupted by the said summons. The messenger referred the King's order to John to join him in London as he required his counsel. To my relief, this time we travelled along the ridgeway by horse. How I prefer land to the sea!

Our first meeting with the Northumbrian nobleman, Uhtred of Bebbanburgh, made a deep impression on me. This warrior, the bravest leader in the North of Angle-land, apprised us of the current situation over ale in a wharf-side tavern. We had found him with difficulty, taxed by the King in London to gain a briefing from his naval commander. Since we could not pursue his ship, the *Sea Eagle*, along the Thames, we had to wait for it to dock to meet the imposing chieftain. His long blond hair, tied behind his neck, reached the middle of his back —a superficial sign of the nobility he exuded in his words, deeds and poise.

Overcoming his diffidence in having to converse with two monks, Uhtred responded to John's acute intelligence by regaling us with his account of recent events.

"After King Alfred took London, two Viking chieftains, the brothers Erik and Sigefrid Thorgilsson, encamped at Two Tree Island at the mouth of the river at Hadleigh. We could not allow that to go unpunished. So, in my role of military governor of London, I commandeered two Mercian warships and came upon the *Sea Eagle*. It's captain, Olaf Eagle-Claw, refused to surrender, so we slew him and his crew and took possession of the ship." So far, he had related this in a matter-of-fact tone, but his weather-beaten face relaxed into a grin, "The invaders of our land must learn that we do not fear them. I raised my flag to the mast-top and sailed past in front of Sigefrid's base. Such was the fame of Olaf that they dared not emerge to fight our three ships." He laughed with justifiable pride.

"What is the situation today, Lord Uhtred?" John asked.

The warrior frowned and weighed his words. "My wish is to attack Benfleet, where the Vikings are encamped, but I have only three vessels. My cousin, Aethelred of Mercia, has fifteen farther up the Thames. I have dispatched messages. Still, he does not come. So as not to give the Vikings reason to venture forth, I sent a warning to them that death was coming to Benfleet." The grim smile and hard eyes of the redoubtable warrior confirmed the reputation he had carved out for himself. I did not doubt that we were in the presence of a charismatic leader.

"I know not why Aethelred makes no move. They say he has returned from fighting Welsh cattle thieves. It may be so, but the situation is dire. This morning, I received a message from our King. That is why I am here." There was no mistaking the bitterness in the nobleman's voice. "I am recalled to London to oversee completion of the fortifications at Southwark." He sighed out heavily, "What the King does not know is that the Norse chieftain, Gunkell Hrodsson, has landed with three-score longships. He has chained some together to block the river to the Saxon fleet, my friends. He aims to seize the silver from Rochester church and monastery." He paused, his eyes flashing. "They will have no easy task, for in recent times our King strengthened the defences. The ditches are deeper while the new wooden ramparts are stout. I know the garrison at Rochester is composed of many warriors. Even so, we must hasten to London to inform Alfred. Come, sup that ale, we must away!"

Once more aboard a ship, though only on the Thames, my stomach had no problem since the nobleman had waited in our company for the incoming tide. Thus, the trip was smooth and swift. Sailing upriver, Uhtred complained to John, "The King will want me and my men to garrison London whilst he dashes off to Rochester, you'll see."

"Ay, but Lord Uhtred, it would be unwise to leave the city unguarded when Vikings are at Benfleet."

"What's to stop them joining Gunkell? Advise the King well, Brother."

Uhtred's prediction proved correct in all senses. After greeting his northern earl with much affection, Alfred ordered him to defend London and goad the labourers at the Southwark fortification to greater effort.

"John, Gwynn, after what Lord Uhtred reported, we must ride into Kent with all haste. I am glad you brought your swords." He trusted his defences to hold out. Meanwhile, Alfred assembled an army of horsemen. Taking the household warriors of every ealdorman in eastern Wessex, the speed of his attack with over a thousand riders took the besieging Vikings by surprise. The early skirmishes at their rear went in our favour until Gunkell raised a flag of truce.

"Why does the King stall?" I asked my fretful friend when I realised that the King was prolonging the parley unnecessarily. With his reply, I discovered the reason for his anxious mood.

"We are waiting for Lord Aethelred and his ships, Brother. They have arrived in London, but do not come. This is our chance to turn the Medway red with Viking blood. They ought to seal off the Norsemen's escape route, but they do not come," he repeated, frustrated.

Gunkell, sensing King Alfred's ruse of delaying, devised a ploy of his own. I admit that it deceived me, too. That evening, I strolled to the edge of our camp and gazed out over the Norse encampment. The campfires burnt brightly, just as Gunkell intended us to observe. They were an artful decoy since he and his men stole away to their ships in the night. They rode the ebb tide into the Thames and fled, evading certain destruction had Aethelred arrived. Still, Rochester had survived, its treasure safe. Our spies informed our furious King that the Danish fleet had split. Some returned to Benfleet; more sailed up the coast to East Anglia; others, we discovered later, headed for Germany. Would there be no end to this Viking scourge?

John soothed the King's rage.

"Sire, in your predecessor's day, with respect, this would not have been the outcome. Your defences held at Rochester. You paid no tribute and the Danes were lucky to escape alive."

"Ah, there's the rub, Brother John! They should not have fled. Lord Aethelred had better have a good excuse."

He did not.

The feeble excuse for not arriving was that his men would not sail as the ale had turned sour. I believe that Alfred's need for Aethelred's support exceeded his wrath, for nobody paid the consequences of such dereliction of duty.

In Winchester, we reported the details of the relief of Rochester to the chroniclers. Scrutinising the scribes' work, we met with an old acquaintance. Bishop Asser had returned to court at the request of Alfred.

Asser might well be the only scholar I ever knew capable of

matching or even superseding John's learning. His unexpected arrival was a source of joy to us both, not shared by the lesser light Brother Esegar. The envious monk failed to understand the importance of Asser to our King. Apart from the depths of his knowledge, his presence at court protected the kingdom from the depredations of the King of Dyfed, who had submitted to Alfred's lordship. Alfred's subsequent generous treatment of Asser festered within Esegar's breast as I shall explain in due course.

King Alfred fended off the Vikings at sea. Despite losing the second battle in the Stour, he defeated the Vikings at London and conceded Lord Aethelred charge of the city. Thus, we enjoyed two years of calm in Winchester, in which we completed our Boethius and revelled in stimulating discussions with our fellow scholars. For the first time, Asser hinted at his project of writing a biography of King Alfred, something I now know he failed to finish because it ends abruptly in 887—some twelve years before our King's death. I suspect that his long sessions with the chroniclers provided him with much of the content as it stands. I know not if he will complete *The Life of King Alfred* because Asser is aged and feeble. None among us knows how long will be granted to us on this Earth. I have survived the Vikings to reach a venerable age, more than can be said for many of my contemporaries. I will now attempt to complete this narrative before the Lord summons me to join my old friend.

NINETEEN

The next few years provided a lull in the Viking incursions, enabling Alfred to advance his learning programme. We finished work on the Boethius only for our King to demand a translation and illustrated version of Saint Augustine's *Soliloquia*. Also, Brother Esegar decided on a period of false cordiality leading to his increased presence in the scriptorium. Intimidated by the strength of my friend's personality, he was wary of John, preferring to concentrate his attention on me. However much he tried to cloak his character with feigned amiability, occasional lapses betrayed him.

One day, he drew near and whispered, "What about Bishop Asser, then?"

"What of him?"

"They say that King Alfred has asked for the bishop's tutelage in Latin. The truth is, there are better Latin scholars available than the Welshman."

The implied referral to himself irritated me. Despite his

jealous nature, Esegar was an outstanding Latinist, but it should be others who praise a man, not oneself.

"Do you not think that tutoring the King is a delicate matter, Brother Gwyn?"

"Why so?"

The wiry monk's thin face pinched even more as he pursed his lips. "The King will soon be forty. Although his mind is active and intelligence acute, it is harder to learn a language when the bloom of youth has passed."

"All the more important that Alfred has chosen someone he is at ease with as a tutor."

Esegar shrugged, scowled, and left me to my paintbrush. The King's choice rankled with him, but not as much as the monarch's next decision. Alfred decided to open a monastic school at the Minster. To do this, he designated different roles to the eminent scholars assembled at his court. John was charged to teach the novices Greek; our ruler assigned me as the Latin teacher; once adequately allotted the whole range of scholastic subjects, Alfred appointed Esegar as the theologian. Brother Esegar came to me fairly bristling but had to rein in his voice lest his resentment became common knowledge.

"The King is unjust!" He whispered close to my ear, "You are a fine illustrator, Brother, but a teacher of *Latin*—it is a travesty!"

What could I say or do? Esegar was right. He was far more proficient in Latin than I, but the King had chosen. That is what I told the outraged monk. His glare informed me that he was unpersuaded of my sincerity while those hate-filled eyes put me on my guard. The royal decision had advantages and disadvantages: the morning teaching commitments meant we needed much longer to finish our book work. On the other hand, Esegar was so offended that he kept away from me, thus not disturbing my concentration with his complaints. Apart from the *Soliloquia*, King Alfred had requested versions of Gregory the Great's *Dialogi* and Bede's *Historia ecclesiastica*. His admirable thirst for the dissemination of learning made the Winchester scriptorium pre-eminent in Wessex if not the foremost in the whole of Angle-land. Indeed, our scribes in those years could match anything the Franks produced.

During this time, King Alfred urged scholars from overseas to come to Winchester. Our scriptorial hive of activity drew them from far and wide. Not all of them came for coin or privileges. Some, like Brother Grimbald, arrived purely out of a love of study, as his refusal of the Archbishopric of Canterbury proved.

"He must be mad," Esegar declared. "Too much reading has impaired his brain."

On the contrary, I admired the scholar for taking his position, whatever his motives. "You must respect a man's choices, Esegar; I am sure he will have taken his decision after deep deliberation."

"Harumph!" The permanently dissatisfied monk stormed out of the scriptorium. As ever, I was pleased to see the back of him. However, with hindsight, I believe the events around Christmas that year were the tipping point for Esegar's warped mind, driving him over the edge to insanity. Already, he was having difficulty coping with the influx of foreign scholars, but he saw King Alfred favour Bishop Asser—a Welshman, hence a foreigner to him—above himself, a Wessex man. On Christmas Eve, 886, after Asser had tried and failed to obtain permission to return to Wales, the King gave him the monasteries of Congresbury and Barnwell with a silk coat and a quantity of incense weighing as much as a stout man. Esegar roamed the cloisters muttering to himself and displaying ill-temper to anyone who drew too close.

Returning to Plegmund, a Mercian former hermit who had

joined us at Winchester, and also translated a Latin version of the *Cura Pastoralis* to rival John's, proved an excellent choice as Archbishop of Canterbury. One of his first acts was to reform the diocese of Winchester, creating four new sees. Esegar dared not criticise this nomination openly, because of Plegmund's sanctity and scholarly renown. This silence did not deceive me. I caught the envious glances and studied reluctance to engage with Plegmund in the period before his consecration.

To heighten Esegar's suppressed rage, a jubilant Bishop Asser shared his joy with us scribes in the spring of 887.

"A triumph, Brothers! This morning"—he waved a sheet of parchment—"our King has read and translated his first Latin passage!"

Except for Esegar, who remained in gloomy silence, we scribes all congratulated Asser on his achievement. Delivered the first of two blows to the lugubrious monk, King Alfred inflicted the second. Gathering John, Esegar, myself and four of his best scribes, our monarch announced,

"Good news, Brothers!" He handed a roll of parchment to John, saying, "Read it later, Abbot." With the formality of his title, I should have realised what was coming. "Building work at the Abbey at Athelney is complete. You all know that Brother John is my choice of abbot and here are four scribes for Athelney. It remains only for me to nominate the Prior. I have given this much thought before deciding it should be a person our abbot is close to and whom he can rely upon for scholarly learning and balanced counsel." I could feel my chest swelling with pride.

The King declared, "Step forward, Prior Esegar."

Strangely, this declaration hit Esegar harder than me. Such was his conceit that he believed he, too, should have an abbey. To be second to John vexed him and gnawed at his innards from that moment. I swallowed my disappointment, which turned instantly to anxiety. The designation of Esegar, I knew instinctively, would lead to trouble. Just how much, I could not suspect that day.

If I thought our transfer to Athelney would relieve us of educational duties, I was mistaken. Given the influx of eager novices, we hardly had time to settle before John, our abbot, announced the formation of a monastic school.

"Prior, you will be teaching Latin, I can think of nobody better qualified."

Esegar immediately scrutinised my face for my reaction but was disappointed because John had forewarned me of his decision. In any case, I saw the correctness of the nomination. Instead, to my delight, my friend named me as the provisioner, that is, the person in charge of the scriptorium. On the announcement, Prior Esegar came to me and offered his congratulations. Though I searched his face for insincerity or hypocrisy, I could find none. Why should there have been when becoming the provisioner was not among his ambitions? Nay, Prior Esegar aimed much higher. So, it came as another devastating blow to his demented mind when later that year, King Alfred gave Asser the monastery of Exeter. To anyone prepared to listen to his hate-filled rantings, Esegar railed against the King's preference for foreigners, whilst all the time overlooking his fellow men of Wessex—namely, the brilliant scholar, Esegar.

Isolated in the Somerset marshes did not mean that we were forgotten or removed from involvement in major events as before. The King needed John's expertise regularly, so whilst my friend filled his limited free time by writing acrostic poems, whenever Alfred required, he presented himself. The first occasion occurred in 888, only three months after our transferral. Alfred had used a Latin compendium of Mosaic Law as the basis for his new code. Soon, he discovered he needed John's advice on which laws to adopt and which to reject.

Shaping his opus on earlier codes, Alfred drew on John's knowledge of the law in Old Saxony to incorporate what pleased him; he did likewise with materials from Kent and Mercia. The result was Alfred's visionary *domboc,* or law code. The most prominent feature was the clause stating the crime, followed by the appropriate punishment: a fine, banishment, scourging, mutilation or death. However severe, there were wise and just provisions for the accused to produce oath helpers to vouch for him and pledge surety or even to undergo an ordeal to verify his guilt or innocence. In the future, Athelney Abbey would be forced to draw upon the contents of the *domboc.*

Determined to bring about a rebirth of the skills lost through the years due to negligence and warfare, King Alfred set aside one-sixth of his annual revenues to the upkeep of craftsmen. The western perimeter of our monastic compound boasted a foundry, a metalworker's shop, chandlery, goldsmith and jeweller's, horn, bone and ivory carver, enamel worker and a smithy. Not all newcomers to the Abbey had a vocation. Many came from overseas at the summons of the King, who had not forgotten his visit with his father to Rome in 855, nor their sojourn at the Frankish court on their return. They came away with a marriage contract and the deep impression of how physical beauty could facilitate spirituality. Thus, Alfred flooded Athelney with craftsmen, precious metals, and jewels. After all, what safer place than the Somerset marshes to manufacture his treasures?

The metalworker boasted a close friendship with Abbot John, I suppose because he had joined us from our native Saxony. Homesickness affects everyone to some extent, so John, being no different in that respect, enjoyed hearing tales of Old

Saxony. Occasionally, he combined my talents with those of Fredegar the bronze-smith. I designed the large candlestick for the Easter candle, the Saxon craftsman faithfully cut the mould and proudly showed us the finished work.

Abbot John lifted the weighty ornament with ease and peered at the wicked spike, devised to pierce the base of the thick candle to hold it in place.

"This might have served in the shield wall at Ethandun," he joked, delicately tapping the sharp point with his forefinger. Instead, I preferred to admire the sprightly animals and geometric motifs arranged in small fields that I had conceived.

"Fredegar, you have honoured my designs to perfection. Bless you!"

"You are the artist, Brother Gwyn, I am merely a carver of moulds."

Regarding candles, our King, too, was inventive. On one visit, he brought two ideas to Fredegar. The first was a design for a lantern which, in jest, he called a *lanthorn* because it was to be made of wood and horn but set on a bronze base and bound with bands. The thin horn was transparent, but protected the candle flame from the wind. The lanthorn was a boon outdoors on a moonless night. The other royal invention was a candle clock. The King came to me first to draw his design on parchment, which proved to be no hard task, for the beauty of the clock lay in its simplicity. Following his description, I drew a wall-mounted candlestick located in a base positioned before a rear panel incised with graduated lines. The receptacle housed a twelve-inch candle that burnt down in four hours. Each line served as a twenty-minute marker—so simple, yet a godsend for Abbot John, whose time had to be jealously apportioned. King Alfred's mind was restless and roved over every aspect of life in his kingdom.

The influx of foreign craftsmen, slaves and monks to

Athelney enriched the Abbey, but was also destined to have a calamitous effect on our lives.

Prior to that, the lull before the storm ended with the frightening arrival to our shores of 330 Viking longships in two divisions. The larger host landed at Appledore in Kent, the lesser army under a chieftain named Hastein in the same shire at Milton. The presence of wives and children within his ships announced the Danes' intention of colonisation.

As soon as the spring weather permitted in 893, King Alfred took up position on a strategic height, chosen by John, whence we could observe both hosts. Ay, the King had commanded us to leave the Abbey to aid him in the face of the Viking threat. As a result, Esegar took over the daily running of our monastery, freeing him to continue his scheming against our abbot.

The amassed forces below us drove such pettiness from our minds. Following John's counsel, Alfred parleyed with Hastein. John rightly believed that the Wessex force was in no position to fight both armies simultaneously.

"Sire, if we can persuade Hastein to withdraw, we can concentrate our might against the larger army."

Profiting from the distraction of the negotiations, the Appledore Danes under Sigurd Bloodhair slipped away towards the north-west. Alfred had wisely held back a Wessex force under the command of his son Edward, who intercepted Sigurd at Farnham, inflicting a heavy defeat and recapturing the plunder. The defeated Vikings fled to take refuge on the island of Thorney on the River Colne.

Informed of the situation, King Alfred turned to John for counsel.

"We should remain in our camp. Soon enough Hastein will learn of Sigurd's losses. We must prepare for his move. Edward should blockade the Norsemen on the island: sooner or later they will sue for peace."

It was sound advice since Sigurd surrendered hostages with a promise to leave Wessex in peace. Viking promises tended to be worthless, as Sigurd proved by marching and plundering in Essex, forcing Edward to react. Hastein had previously built a fortress in the marshland near London at Benfleet where Sigurd joined him. Together they left the fortress on a raid, allowing Edward to storm it by surprise. The Wessex force destroyed some of the Danish fleet, breaking up some ships, burning others, and capturing and taking yet more to Rochester.

Before these events, an envoy arrived when our army was about to march to relieve Edward at the blockade of Thorney.

"Lord"—the breathless messenger bowed—"Vikings! They have raised a great force from the settlements in East Anglia and Northumbria."

"Where are they?" Alfred's patience snapped.

The rider paled, gathered his wits and replied, "Sire, they sailed around the coast into the Channel and attacked Devon. There, they built a fortress and then surrounded Exeter. The burh is holding out, but the food is scarce."

"John?"

"Send for aid to your thegns in Wessex and across the borders, Sire. Ay, even into Wales. Have them raise men to march into Devon. We can leave Edward to deal with these Vikings. After Farnham, he has enough men to cope with the combined Danish forces."

John's advice proved sound again, so we set off on a forced ride to Devon. The King, wisely, took only his mounted force across the country. Time was of the essence, but the dispatches had been effective. The King's thegns managed to assemble a great army consisting of both Saxons and Welshmen. The combined army laid siege to the Vikings who had built a fortification at Buttington. We turned the tables on the Northmen not only by relieving Exeter, but also pursuing the enemy and entrapping them in their stronghold. After several weeks the starving Vikings broke out of their fortress. We were ready. At last, John and I found ourselves again in a shield-wall, but this time alongside the Welsh, who are hardy, valiant fighters. After hours of wearisome combat, we prevailed to put the Vikings to flight. It was in that fight that I obtained the scar that runs down my left cheek. Luckily for me, I didn't lose an eye that day.

Although the Danes still infested the Thames Valley, the crisis was over. King Alfred would have little peace until the end of his reign, but as John pointed out, "Lord, the worst is passed. May we return to our monastic duties?"

Royal approval granted, we returned to Athelney and unforeseen troubles.

TWENTY

Before reaching the heart of my narrative, indulge an old man in some reflection. I first came to my conclusions about the importance of culture when I came face to face with an angry thegn. In our society, the firstborn son inherits his father's land and assumes his obligations and responsibilities.

One day, a Wiltshire thegn, father of three sons, unwillingly crossed the causeway with his eldest. He stated his problem to Abbot John. I happened to be present in the abbot's quarters in my role of provisioner.

After introducing himself as Thegn Ernulf of Tilshead in the hundred of Whorwellsdown, a place in Wiltshire near the Somerset border, he launched into his tirade.

"This is my eldest son, Wolfram. I have taught him all I know—combat, riding, hunting. In short, all he needs is to take over my lands when I am gone. My lad is a hearty fighter; none of his peers can match him."

Gazing upon the broad shoulders and muscular limbs, I could see why the youth might be all his father claimed, but he stood there, his face a picture of sorrow as his father continued his rant.

"Now that I have prepared him and he's of an age to fight beside our King against the Viking raiders, how does he repay me? All I can get out of him is that he wants to be a monk, to learn to read and write. But I ask you, Father Abbot," he said as he sent a defiant glare towards John, "when did learning ever put bread on the table?"

At that point, John turned to indicate me. I had remained silent and standing still near the wall behind my abbot.

"Thegn Ernulf, look at this monk's face." The left side under the eye down to my beard was slashed by an angry red line where the flesh was healing from a cut inflicted by a Viking blade at Buttington. "A Viking sword nigh on took his sight. Were you at Buttington, Thegn?"

"I was that!" the nobleman replied proudly. "We sent the raiders to join their pagan gods!"

"So, you see, being a monk does not necessarily mean renouncing the defence of what you believe in," said my wise Superior. "I, too, was at that battle, fighting next to my King."

"*You?*" said the warrior with an air of doubt.

"Have a care, my friend," John boomed. "Appearances may deceive." He reached under his desk and pulled forth his sword, peacefully sheathed. But only for a moment, because the next, the bare blade was under the thegn's chin.

"Father Abbot," said Wolfram, "put away your weapon. I think you have convinced my father." The handsome youth displayed not only charm and intelligence, but an admirable loyalty.

"Ay, but what of my estates?" the thegn asked.

"Father, you have two other sons. Arfrid can almost hold his own in combat with me. You are strong, sire. When you are old, he will care for you and manage the lands. Besides, you never know, I may become an abbot!"

No sooner had he said that than he flushed and begged forgiveness of John, who, however, had seen something in the youth that impressed him so favourably that he limited himself to: "There is much for you to learn even before you are accepted as a simple monk, my friend."

"Father, I have a thirst for learning!"

The potentially rancorous encounter ended amicably, with Thegn Ernulf promising money to the Abbey to contribute to his son's upkeep. This was not an imposition but an unprompted and appreciated act of generosity. Like father like son, I thought, understanding where the youth had obtained his manners.

This brief yet instructive encounter set me to thinking on a broader scale. The words spoken in anger remained for days in my head: *when did learning ever put bread on the table?* We had lived through recent hard winters of shortages and famine. I thought about what the Vikings wanted—wealth without toil or the best fertile soil; also, about why we had risked our lives to defend our land. I gingerly ran my fingers down my offended cheek. A wider vision opened up my horizons—King Alfred saw farther than I, but suddenly I glimpsed something too. *Culture is the identity of the nation.* Young Wolfram sought learning rightly: he yearned for something his elders had not transmitted to him. Culture is shared through language and is a continuous slow process, but it teaches us to think, not individually but by providing the concept of the family and nation. King Alfred had realised this when he reached his lowest point, hidden in the marshes of Somerset with a whole way of life, an entire Saxon culture, under threat. The King did not limit his vision to books and words, trust me —as a man of artistic inclination, I am well placed to underline this. Culture can be expressed in material objects, not only in writing.

My reflection over, I continue with my tale and despite appearances, there is a connection with my contemplation.

Since the earliest days in Athelney, Abbot John acquired the habit of silent nocturnal meditation in the empty church. His routine was not common knowledge which, as a lover of solitude, he preferred. I recount this unfortunate episode as he told it to me. One night, in the late spring of 894, as usual, he left his quarters at three in the morning, crossed the courtyard and ambled unsuspectingly down the silent nave to kneel before the altar in prayer. Halfway through the *Pater Noster*, he broke off, alarmed to hear a shuffling from the back of the church. Leaping to his feet, he turned around to see three villains armed with swords rushing down the aisle towards him.

Unarmed, he realised that he was in a situation of mortal danger. Glancing around and, as ever a quick thinker, he seized the Easter candlestick and instinctively used it as a club to fend away the first assailant. At the same time, his deep voice boomed and echoed around the church as he called for help. When he warded off the second blow with the heavy ornament, he remembered the cast spike still impaling the thick candle stub. Working frantically to detach the wax, he received his first wound to his side. Enraged, he threw the stub to the ground then swung the candlestick around to make the spike an effective weapon. In doing so, he suffered a second wound and began to feel dizzy from loss of blood.

Again, he cried out for help, but unfortunately used the word *devils*. Something along the lines of *Will nobody save me from these devils?* Alas, even at Athelney there are more ignorant than wise monks. Hearing that word, several brothers alerted by the abbot's cries hesitated for fear of demons, so failed to enter the church out of superstitious terror. The delay gave John time to impale one of the villains with the spike, but also for him to receive another worse wound to his chest. Luckily, the youthful Brother Wolfram arrived and valiantly, fearing neither devil nor man, barged past the cowards to enter the church with a war-cry. The two remaining scoundrels, swords raised over their victim now forced onto one knee, no longer had the abbot's death as their priority, but their escape. The building had a side door through which they fled before Wolfram reached them. He had time only to recognise them as slaves brought to Athelney by Frankish dealers.

With a presence of mind, he sent for our infirmarian who, as God would have it, is a skilled healer. He refused to move John from the church, ordering the monks to bring a bed into the building. I am sure this consideration saved my friend's life, because it enabled the staunching of the wounds. Wolfram armed himself with a sword; together with a small group of friends, they went to the slaves' quarters where they ascertained the unexplained absence of three men. At this point, it was clear to Wolfram that two criminals were hiding. A search of the Abbey buildings and grounds proved fruitless, so as dawn broke he led an armed party across the causeway where, using his undoubted intelligence and instincts, he took his band of seekers into the marshes. Soon, his hunting skills drew his attention to tell-tale signs: a freshly broken reed, a waterfilled footprint, and so on. Before long, movement among the sedges alerted one of the hunters. After a short skirmish, one of the fugitives received an incapacitating wound to his sword arm. The other threw down his weapon and surrendered. They brought them back to the Abbey.

Prior Esegar had them imprisoned in a strongroom then, curiously, entered alone where he remained for some time. When he emerged, he gave instructions that nobody was to speak to the prisoners on any account. The prior placed two guards at the door and repeated the order, stressing it for their benefit. The hypocrite organised a Mass to pray for the swift recovery of the abbot.

Wolfram, knowing about my closeness to our Father Superior, came to the vestry where they had transported the invalid's bed. He knew that he would find me there at my friend's side. John's fever had subsided, so the signs were that he would make a return to health.

"Brother Gwyn," said the young monk, "there's something most suspicious about this situation."

"What do you mean?" I kept my voice low to match his.

"Why would three slaves wish to attack the abbot? I can think of no reason unless ..."

I had been too worried about my friend to think along those lines, but now that he mentioned it, I finished his thought with, "Unless someone wished to profit by his death."

"Quite so. Isn't it peculiar that the prior insisted that nobody should question the criminals? I asked the guards and they confirmed that the prisoners had not received food or water. Brother Gwyn, two days without food and drink! He means to starve them."

This affirmation came as a revelation: *Esegar is covering his tracks.*

"Come, Wolfram. Let's fetch our swords and hope not to use them. I'll obtain bread and water."

So doing, we met in the courtyard before striding to the building where the prisoners were enclosed.

"Open the door," I commanded. "The prior's orders," I lied.

Eyeing the bread and water, the older of the guards nodded, took a key and turned it in the lock.

"Wait outside," I murmured to Wolfram, so that only he could hear, "make sure that you warn me if anything untoward happens." I knew that I could rely on that exceptional young fellow.

Inside, dispensing bread and water, I saw that the wounded man was in a bad way. "You need the infirmarian," I said, gazing at the man's discoloured arm. His companion had roughly bound the wound, but the cloth did not cover the gravity of the condition. I helped the slave to his feet. How I loathed the all-too-common practice of enslavement. "I will take you to the healer."

Draping his sound arm around my shoulder, I lugged the helpless captive out of the cell. Outdoors, the guard made to protest, but I said calmly, "I'm taking him to the infirmary. He's too weak to escape, friend. I'll take full responsibility."

The stench the wound emitted upon its unbinding warned the infirmarian of the first stages of putrefaction.

"Just in time, Brother Gwyn. Another day and he would have lost his arm, at the least. As it is, I think I can cure him."

"Good. Keep a close watch on him, Brother. He must not flee. I will send an armed man to guard him." I did not have far to stroll before meeting Brother Wolfram.

"I want you to stand over the prisoner in the infirmary. Do not allow anyone, especially not the Prior, to move him. If you can get a confession out of him, make sure he repeats it to the infirmarian."

That is what happened. The offender, a Slav, grateful for the treatment to his arm and, above all, eager to save his hide, confessed to Wolfram along these lines: "The Prior promised us our liberty and a handsome recompense if we managed to slay the abbot at night. He told us that Abbot John would be there to pray when the building was empty. All we had to do was conceal ourselves in the darkness at the back of the church then surprise him at prayer. We wanted our freedom, Brother. The Prior promised it with silver coin; he also provided the swords."

Faithful to my request, Wolfram had the man repeat his accusation to the infirmarian. The elderly healer, a lifetime of devotion to his calling, reacted with outrage.

"That serpent! What can we do? He is in charge of the Abbey while the abbot is weak. We must not trouble the patient with this."

"Ay, but neither can we allow Prior Esegar to silence the witnesses. I know just the man to deal with this situation."

Wolfram turned to the wounded man and said, "Do not worry, despite your serious crime. If you are willing to speak out in public ... if you repeat to the brothers what you have told us, you may yet obtain your freedom. Wait here. Trust me—do not attempt to flee. I must set the wheels of justice in motion." He came to me in the scriptorium, the ideal place for what I had in mind. Rapidly, I wrote a summons for the arrest of Prior Esegar. Carrying the sheet of parchment, ink, and a quill to the vestry, I had Wolfram repeat the slave's statement to John.

"Sign this warrant, John. I'll have Esegar arrested at once."

I dipped the pen in the ink, passing the quill to my friend who, helped by the young monk, had propped himself on his elbow to sign. Surprisingly firmly, he signed his name with a flourish.

No sooner had the ink dried than I beckoned Wolfram to come with me. I showed the document to the guards at the strongroom door.

"Leave your post. Come with me to arrest the prior. That fiend is responsible for the attack on our beloved abbot."

The older of the two sentinels objected. "How is it possible? What proof do you have, Brother Gwyn?"

"All that serves. We have the confession of one of the attackers and quite probably will have his too, soon enough." I pointed to the locked door. "Let's waste no more time. Esegar is the instigator. We must arrest him."

The guard's eyes narrowed, which bothered me, but it was his way of considering.

"So, the prior wanted to become abbot, did he? We'll see about that!"

Relieved at his acceptance of the truth, I led the three men armed with swords to the abbot's quarters where Esegar had installed himself.

I did not knock but threw the door open and stormed into the room.

"What is the meaning of this?" Esegar attempted to sound authoritative, but his voice quavered. The three unsheathed swords had unmanned him.

"I have a warrant, signed by the abbot, for your arrest, Prior Esegar," said the foremost guard.

"Don't be ridiculous! On what charge? Is the abbot delirious?"

"We have the confession of a man you instigated to the crime of murder, Prior."

"Absurd. Are you going to take the word of a slave over that of a prior?"

"How do you know it is a slave who confessed? I did not mention it."

"Obvious—we captured the slaves who are trying to save their skins by shifting the blame. A prior is an easy target as next in line to run the Abbey." He was an able advocate of himself, but I was having none of it.

"Guards, seize him! Lock him in the strongroom he chose for his henchmen."

"This is an outrage! The King appointed me. I'll see you all punished for this."

"Not if God judges you guilty, Prior." An idea was forming in my mind.

Some minutes later, Prior Esegar, alone in his cell, was still falsely pleading his innocence whilst the other Slav, now in the open, confirmed his fellow conspirator's tale. Having heard him out, I returned to the prior's cell. Leaning close to the door, I called, "It is your choice of strongroom and guards, Prior. Shall I also follow your example of food and drink?"

From within came a whining reply, "Nay, nay I beg you, have mercy!"

I turned away in disgust.

"See that he has water and something to eat at the regular meal times. He will remain under constant guard until the Abbot recovers enough to resume his duties. Abbot John will see that justice is done."

All that remained for the moment was a conversation with my friend about King Alfred's law code. A particular clause stuck in my memory—I wished to share it with the abbot.

TWENTY-ONE

ATHELNEY, SPRING, 894 AD

During the following days, we transported John in his bed from the gloomy vestry to the comfort of his quarters. I deserted my scriptorial duties to sit by him and respond to his requests or to distract him with conversation.

"What of Esegar?" he asked.

"What of him? He awaits trial when you are back on your feet."

The abbot lay there considering the ceiling, before slowly saying, "The King's law states that the good of the state is a harmony of love and justice."

I stared at my friend so hard that he could not hold my eyes and turned his head on his bolster.

How could he talk blithely of love and justice as he lay sorely wounded? Wounds inflicted on the orders of a man who should have been faithful to him. Nay, it would not do! I rose and crossed to his crowded bookshelves. It took me a while to find what I wanted. Finally, my finger rested on the *domboc*— Alfred's law code. A glance revealed that John's breathing was even; he had surrendered to the sleep his body craved for healing.

The abbot's slumber suited me well, leaving me seated at his desk with the law code, unchallenged by John's restless mind. I read as quickly as I dared, for I did not wish to miss anything of importance. For that reason, I did not skip past the King's Preface. I'm glad I did not, because at the very end of the section, after long consideration of Mosaic law and various references to the Old Testament, the King concluded, *all offences are to be treated in mitigating fashion, all except treason against one's lord*. I read the passage again. Ay, it was clear: the Scriptures stated that the person of one's lord is inviolate. The lord of Prior Esegar was his abbot. Moving on into the body of the code that dealt with particular crimes, I came to Cap. 4. I seized a pen and sheet of vellum, copying the article word for word. John would be able to hold a page of parchment, but not a heavy volume. Here is the transcription:

> *Whoever intentionally kills a man, let him die the death. Whoever kills a man out of necessity or unwillingly or unwittingly, as God gave him into his hand, and he did not ambush him, let him be responsible for the life and its legal compensation, if he seeks sanctuary. If someone then kills his neighbour desirefully and intentionally through cunning, remove him from my altar that he may die the death.*

There could be no argument. Esegar had set a trap to ambush and slay his abbot—the punishment was death.

When John woke, I gave him water for his parched lips. After some small-talk, I reported my findings, stepping over to his desk to bring him the short transcription. He read it and sighed deeply.

185

"Yet, I do not feel that it is my place to judge a man, Gwyn."

I bit my tongue to avoid snapping at him. Here was a man who had slain Vikings in battle: why this compunction for a treacherous prior? After a calculated silence, enough to master my feelings, I said, "Prior Esegar will have a hard task persuading anyone that he had no criminal intent to secret ambush."

John's countenance clouded. "Ay, that he will. But you miss my point, Gwyn. I do not wish to sit in judgement when a man's life is at stake."

"Give me more time with the King's laws, Father Abbot," I said formally. Steadily, I worked my way through the tome until an implicit clause, in this case referring to a confirmation of King Ine's law, inspired me. I took up the argument again with the invalid.

"Abbot John, you do not want to *sit in judgement* over Esegar's fate. I presume you have no objection to God deciding his guilt or innocence? If you appoint me to conduct the trial given your temporary indisposition, I will adhere strictly to the King's laws and God's decision."

His face was ashen, so I bitterly regretted overtaxing him. To my joy, he said, "So be it, Brother Asher"— this use of my real name revealed the precarious state of his health.

I kissed his brow. "Very well, old friend. Tomorrow, I will make the preparations and conduct the trial."

"A *fair* trial, mark you!"

"I give you my word, John. On my oath"—I moved to his lectern and placed my hand on the Bible—"I swear on the Holy Book."

Straight after Prime the next morning, I arranged for workers to construct a temporary hearth in the nave before the altar. At my bidding, the same men brought wood and coal to lay ready for a fire. On my instructions, two cooks fetched a large iron cauldron from the kitchen, which they positioned on a metal tripod over the fuel. From the well, monks carried five buckets of water so the cauldron was two-thirds full. To end the arrangements, I summoned the brothers to the church where a priest performed a purification ceremony of the building and the onlookers. The rite concluded; I ordered the fire lit. Both doors of the sacred edifice opened wide ensured a strong draught that fanned the flames and swept away the smoke.

As I waited for the water to boil, I took the abbot's place to explain to the monks what was happening.

"Brothers, we have proof that Prior Esegar plotted to murder Abbot John. Today, you will witness the trial of the accused man, for God, not Man, will decide his fate. If found guilty, the penalty is death."

At these words, there was a growl of approbation, for John was a popular abbot and Esegar equally disliked. One or two of the older Saxon monks resented having a foreign superior, but they represented a small minority. I stepped down to stroll up to the cauldron. Peering over the rim of the iron vessel, I withdrew my head rapidly from the scalding steam. The tumult of bubbles meant the time to conduct the trial had come.

"Fetch the prior," I called to Wolfram, who was waiting for this order by the door. "Strip him to the waist!"

A few minutes later, down the aisle stumbled the scrawny, half-naked figure of the detestable prior. His ribs stood out stark, unprotected by fat or muscles. Fixed on the steaming cauldron, his pinched visage seemed all frightened as I gazed upon him. Without pity, I announced the accusation, citing the witnesses and quoting Cap. 4 from the King's code.

"Witnesses!" Esegar screamed, "Two foreign slaves! In any case, the abbot is not my lord—the King is!"

In this way, he sought to avoid justice, but I was irremovable. "Prior Esegar, do you see this stone?" I held up a smooth river rock from my desk, used as a paperweight. I lobbed it into the boiling water. "God will be your judge today. If you are innocent, as you claim, He will protect you. Your task is to seek and remove the stone from the cauldron with your right hand."

The depth of the water was calculated to reach beyond his elbow.

"What are you waiting for? Are you not eager to prove your innocence?"

The hypocrite crossed himself while his lips moved in silent prayer. I doubt God was listening to him. But if He had been, He could not have failed to hear the sinner's agonised screams as his arm plunged into the boiling water. Moments later, he withdrew it, his face screwed in agony, which emotion he then replaced with a triumphant sneer. "See, I am innocent." He passed the rock to me. Again, I lobbed it into the cauldron.

"How many slaves did you corrupt to murder our abbot?"

"None," he lied, cradling his scalded arm.

"Three, Prior, *three* men with swords against an unarmed older man. Therefore, it is a threefold test such as, by the way, the King's code provides for, in each of which you must retrieve the rock. Go again with the same hand."

The coward tried to turn and run, but Wolfram's strong hand caught him by the shoulder and hauled him to the cauldron. "You heard the Provisioner," he hissed between clenched teeth. "Go on, or I'll shove your head in there instead!"

That would have been a crime, but the threat was enough. Esegar thrust his arm into the bubbling liquid once more, screamed, and pulled it out without the stone.

"That is not valid," I said. "You must withdraw the rock. Again!"

The disgraced prior whimpered and from the corner of his

eye saw Wolfram draw his sword, which persuaded him to plunge his arm desperately into the boiling water. The limb remained immersed for ten heartbeats as he howled like a wounded wolf before emerging with the stone.

"Good. One last time Esegar, then it is over." I tossed the rock back into the water.

His words, hard to understand with his sobbing, amounted to, "Nay, Bother Gwynn, enough! Have mercy!"

"The same mercy you showed to Abbot John? So be it! Retrieve the rock or be sentenced to death!"

He howled an unrepeatable blasphemy, followed by a curse so that Wolfram cuffed him viciously across his ear. "Again!" cried the youthful monk.

Once more, he groped around for the smooth stone, at last throwing himself on the paved floor, tears streaming down his face. The rock fell rolling and clattering from his hand.

"Infirmarian! Bind the arm. It will remain covered for three days. When you remove the binding, if the arm is unscathed, God has decreed his innocence; on the other hand, if the arm festers, he is guilty and condemned to die for his crime. Take him to his cell."

Wolfram and another monk had to hoist him out of the church, because he had fainted from his ordeal.

"Brothers, we will now pray that God, in His mercy, will reveal a just sentence."

The priest managed to make such a simple sentiment last ten minutes, enunciating countless appropriate passages from the Old Testament. Some of the brothers displayed restlessness, no doubt aquiver to be outdoors to discuss the trial. Instead, every citation our priest made comforted me that I had applied the letter, not just of Alfred's law, but more importantly, of God's.

What I wanted most at that moment was to hasten to the

abbot to relate the event. First, however, I supervised the restoration of the nave to its former pristine state. In a short time, the cauldron, ashes, and hearth removed, monks set about scrubbing the paving stones. When the floor had dried, I knelt where the cauldron had stood and prayed for forgiveness. Only I and God knew how I had gloried in Esegar's suffering. This brief oration was not enough; I would have to seek out the priest to confess my sin. Only after Esegar's sentence, I decided, would I do that. Rising, I strode out of the church determined not to give Abbot John any insight into my sinfulness.

After I had recounted my detailed report of the trial, its preparation, execution and corollary cleansing without betraying any emotion, my acute friend asked, "What are you hiding from me, Gwyn?"

Startled, I sought for a suitable reply. "Nothing, Father, except perhaps I am satisfied that God's and the King's will has been done. Or, at least, in three days it will be."

"Gwyn, Gwyn, I know you too well!" He sank back onto his bolster and closed his eyes with an enigmatic smile on his face. I made an excuse to leave. Outside the building, I came upon Wolfram, who stood with his head bowed in contemplation.

"What ails you, Brother?" I asked.

"Ah, Brother Gwyn! Was that justice, Brother?"

"What do you mean?"

"Well, no flesh can survive water that hot. Esegar's arm is bound to fester."

"Unless he is innocent," I replied.

"Do you believe that, Brother?"

"Of course, I am a monk. I believe if it is God's will, Esegar's arm will be unscathed."

The young monk brightened. "I suppose I find it hard to credit that the prior is guiltless." He laughed bitterly, looked serious, and said, "How is Father Abbot?"

"Mending, but he needs to regain strength."

"Is he eating?"

"This evening, the infirmarian will decide if he can manage something more solid than chicken broth."

I am convinced that despite the pain of his wounds, John slept better than I that night. My thoughts raced ahead two days to when Esegar's arm would be unbound. What then? I expected proof of his guilt. What if he was unscathed? The monks demanded justice. In that case, the two slaves would die. What if his wound festered? How would Esegar meet his end? To my surprise, the battle-hardened warrior that I was, I could not sleep for the same scruples that afflicted the abbot. As I tossed and turned in my bed, I concluded that I did not want the miserable Esegar's blood on my hands or my conscience.

What then?

The chiming of the Prime bell came as a relief. On my way to the church, I threw several cupped hands full of the icy well water into my face.

"Bad night, Brother?" The cheerful face of Brother Wolfram grinned into mine.

"Ay, the fate of Prior Esegar disturbed my sleep."

"Mine, too," confessed the youthful monk. As I raised an eyebrow, he added, "I had to rise, kneel, and seek guidance in prayer before my cross nailed to the wall."

The chiming bells became insistent in my head, so I linked arms and steered him towards the Church of St Aethelwine. "How so, Brother Wolfram?"

The monk puffed out his cheeks and released his breath.

"It's like this: I love Abbot John as if he were my father. I burn with the desire to kill that scrawny, evil prior. The man's a traitor! My hatred has nothing to do with justice. Don't you see, Brother?"

I understood only too well. The lad might as well have been expressing *my* sentiments.

As we mounted the steps into the building, my ears battered by the incessant clamour of the bells, I could not think clearly. Not until they ceased and the service began was I able to ponder. I am ashamed to state that I followed nothing of the Mass that morning as my tormented mind again had to wrestle with moral issues. A series of cascading *what-ifs* raced through my head until, finally, I settled on waiting to see whether God decreed the prior's guilt. Although, I would not recognise it—I had decided for every possible outcome.

Today, years later as I narrate this, I stand by my decision and would do the same again.

Before the priest gave his benediction and the dismissal, I caught his eye with two gestures.

Quick on the uptake, the priest announced, "Brothers, I believe the Provisioner wishes to address you."

What an unusual feeling for me to have all eyes and ears at my disposal for the second time in three days.

"Friends, this morning we anxiously await the Almighty's judgement on our prior. I ask you all to congregate in front of the well after the service. Be not rowdy, but prayerful: men's lives are at stake."

The priest reiterated the importance of prayer, spoke briefly of God's mercy, then blessed and dismissed the congregation. To my satisfaction, the monks trooped out of the church, heads bowed in silence. I hoped that everything else would proceed as well.

"Brother Wolfram, go to your room and fetch your sword!"

He looked more gratified than startled as he hurried away.

The monks formed up in orderly fashion before the well. Someone had raised the bucket and was dipping the pewter drinking vessel into the cold water. The sight of the pail that had filled the cauldron reminded me of the task in hand. I ordered for the two trembling slaves to be brought into the courtyard—whatever the judgement, they would be involved. Next, I called the infirmarian to my side, which set off a murmur of conversation among the respectful brothers.

We two senior monks waited for Wolfram to join us. When he arrived, striding towards us, I recognised the look in his eyes. It was an expression shared by men about to go into battle. That wild-eyed look meant I needed not to inquire how he felt about dispensing justice. Whatever the state of Esegar's arm, Wolfram would need his blade. Someone had to pay for what had befallen my best friend.

At my command, the guards opened the cell so that the skinny prior emerged blinking into the daylight.

"Unbind his arm and refer its condition to me, Brother Infirmarian."

The elderly monk unpinned the bandage and to the accompaniment of the groans and cries of the captive, he peeled away cloth and flesh with the same action. The horrible bleeding state of the blistered and festering limb decreed the prior's doom.

"Guilty!" I cried, most likely exultingly to my shame. I turned to Wolfram. "Escort him to the well and execute the sentence, Brother."

Wolfram grasped the struggling prior by the neck, the firmness of the tightening grip halting the writhing. Matching the slow pace of the condemned man, we ambled towards the assembled monks. At the sight of his arm, the brothers began to hiss and hurl insults at the trembling Esegar. I raised a hand for silence to make my announcement.

"God in His wisdom has decreed that Prior Esegar is responsible for the murderous assault on our beloved abbot who even now lies recovering from the grave wounds inflicted on him. In the name of the Father Almighty, I declare Prior Esegar guilty and sentence him to beheading. But first, he may confess his sin to our priest."

The confessor came over, but Esegar raised his head and with an evil expression declared, "This is not justice; I have nought to confess!"

To the outrage of the assembled monks, the miscreant dared to spit at the priest, who wiped his face in disgust. I nodded to Wolfram whose sword was already unsheathed. He shoved Esegar with considerable force between the shoulder blades so that the scoundrel sprawled to the ground. As he attempted to rise, in a flash of steel, the honed blade sliced through the neck: a magnificently clean blow. The head of the monk, who had caused me nothing but offence from the day we had first met, rolled three times towards my feet, its hate-filled eyes glaring.

I placed a sandal on his ear, steepled my hands, and in a ringing voice declared, "God's will be done!"

The congregation chorused, "Amen!"

All faces turned to me for a further announcement. I chose ten monks.

"The man is a condemned murderer: take his body and fling it in the marsh. He shall not be buried in hallowed ground."

The monks looked at each other wordlessly, but I could sense the general understanding and hear the loud murmur of assent owing to the gravity of the crime.

"As for the men who wielded the swords, they will await the return of the man they abused to pronounce his judgement on them. Take them to the holding cell. Feed and water them at mealtimes."

One of the hardest days of my life had come to an end. In old age, I have no regrets, but many reflections upon envy, liberty, and justice. Let Esegar's fate be an example: it is how we respond to life's challenges that distinguish us as men.

TWENTY-TWO

If in my narrative I have failed to convey John's intellect, I can do no better than quote our friend, Bishop Asser, who in his *Life of Alfred,* wrote of him: "a man of most acute intelligence, immensely learned in all fields of literary endeavour, and extremely ingenious in many other forms of expression." Let me add to this a small incident that occurred during the abbot's convalescence.

One morning, he asked for some sheets of parchment, and pen and ink. At the time, I wondered why he needed them. Later in the day, on my return to his quarters, I discovered the reason. His body required time to heal, which was why I found him asleep, but his mind was ever active.

Three pages with writing lay on the floor by the bed next to the ink and quill. I picked up the one with the fewest lines. I will have it copied now as I read it then:

En tibi discendant e celo Gratiae tot Æ

Letus eris semper Ælfred per competa ate L
Flectas iam mentem sacris satiare sirela F
Recte doces properans falsa dulcidine mure R
Ecce aptas clara semper lucrare taltan E
Docte peregrine transcurrere rura sophie D

Of course, I noticed the acrostic at once, but shame on me that I did not spot the telestich immediately—that is, the word composed by the line endings. Remember that this was the shortest of the three acrostic poems on the floor, and you gain an insight into the intelligence of my friend. I will supply a translation in English in the appendix to my narrative.

A man may be intelligent, but for the full measure of his worth look to how he uses that gift. Some months after finding the poems, the abbot rose from his sickbed and threw himself energetically into the running of the monastery. After catching up on the most pressing matters, he remembered the two captives who had attacked him. They had remained in the cell for three months pending his recovery.

"Gwyn, I am returned to health. It is time to deal with the wretches who set upon me."

"What will you do with them? We executed Esegar."

"Rightly so, for his was the wicked mind behind the attack."

I sensed that my friend, despite the suffering he had been through, intended to show mercy. I protested: "But the three ruffians attacked you, an unarmed man, with swords. It was a cowardly assault thwarted only by your quick thinking and the arrival of Wolfram."

"Have them brought to me here in my room, Brother."

The sight of the two prisoners, despite my loathing for them, moved me to pity. Blinking in the strong July sunlight, they covered their eyes until they adjusted to the midday light after the darkness of the strongroom whence they staggered, unused to exercise. Altogether, they cut a pathetic figure, looking like ghouls—undernourished though not starved, their faces drawn with fear. Rightly, they feared the abbot's wrath, for they could not know that he was a true Christian. Even so, John had a wilful streak in his character, which he displayed that morning.

I noticed the sword strapped to his belt as soon as I entered the room.

"Ah, these are the men who attempted to murder me when I was unarmed at prayer. Kneel!"

The two quaking captives exchanged glances and wasted no time in obeying. John's headstrong vein gained the upper hand: he drew his sword.

"Now the situation is reversed," he thundered. "I have my blade while you are weaponless. How does it feel?"

"Mercy, Lord," one of the wretches begged.

"The same mercy you showed me?" John unconsciously echoed the words I had used with Prior Esegar. The abbot continued, prolonging their agony, "You were both present at the trial and execution of your paymaster, is it not so?"

No reply came from the terrified prisoners. I imagine their memories were reliving the sight of the rolling head—I know that mine was.

"Yet," said John, his voice changing to a gentler tone, "Brother Gwyn, we have fought against mercenaries in Frankia. A man *will* fight for money."

"Ay, but those hirelings came up against men with weapons and armour. They were not cowards."

"True," replied the abbot, warming to the debate—how he loved verbal sparring. "But there is something more than coin that motivates a man."

I believe that, at that moment, the older of the two

scoundrels understood that there was hope for their worthless lives. I played my part, knowing he needed a question to expound his point.

"What is that, Abbot John?"

"*Liberty*, Brother. They were slaves and yearned for a return to freedom. The evil Esegar exploited their longing. Remember this, when liberty dies in the heart of a man, no law, no court, can save it. The wretches, ruled by hopelessness, would have done anything to regain their freedom. As things stand, today," said my wise Superior, "these men wish only for a just master. Their liberty is a secondary desire." His eyes met those of the older captive and held them whilst he sheathed his sword.

"Are you Christians?" he asked.

"Nay." One of the Slavs shook his head.

"Well, I am abbot here and have your lives in my hand. It is no sin for me to execute two unrepentant would-be murderers and pagans to boot; my religion, however, teaches me to turn the other cheek. Believe me when I tell you that education is a better safeguard of liberty than a fyrd prepared for battle. I am disposed to spare your lives, ay, and also grant your freedom, on one condition." As usual, John waited for the question.

"What is that, Lord?" the older captive dared to ask.

"You will agree to abandon your heathen gods and embrace our faith with baptism. If you study our beliefs and satisfy Brother Gwyn, who will be your sponsor, before the altar I will grant your freedom."

The strangest thing occurred. The younger of the two, still on his knees, crawled on all fours up to John and kissed his foot. The other raised his head to say, "Lord, we are deeply sorry for our sins. You are a *just master*. I regret raising a hand against you. We will do as you say."

The matter settled, I had learnt another lesson from my

association with the great man. Regarding that, no sooner had he dismissed the two gladdened men than, turning to me, he said, "Well, Prior Gwyn, I consider that to be a very satisfactory conclu—"

"Wait a minute! What did you say?"

"Ay, that's right! *Prior* Gwyn. I'm going to need a replacement. So, who better? You have shown your worth during my sickness. Besides, you can easily combine the priorship with your duties as Provisioner, because I intend to be an ever-present abbot."

More or less, that is what he managed to do in the latter phase of his long life. Apart from witnessing some royal charters: the last one I can recall was for King Edward in the final year of John's life.

Again, I hasten ahead of myself, but not by much. King Alfred visited Athelney whenever he sought John's literary or military advice. He was a kind king and, knowing of John's failing health, did not impose travel on him.

I think the end of my narrative should embrace the two of them: monarch and scholar. As I have stated previously, King Alfred was aware of the importance of Lundenwic and the old fortress of Londinium, and thus recaptured it from the Vikings. By strengthening the defences of the city, then handing it to the Lord of Mercia, Aethelred, Alfred freed himself to deal with the eastern frontier of Mercia. After discussions with John and others, the King decided to wed his daughter, Aethelflaed, to the Lord of Mercia, effectively reducing Aethelred to vassalage. At this point, Alfred received submission from everyone not subject to the Danelaw as King of all the English.

I would, therefore, like to dwell a little on the matter of paradox. Strange, is it not, that the King who had the wit to call upon foreigners like John, Asser, Grimbald, and myself, not always with consensus, to further a rebirth of learning in the land, should thereby instil a sense of nation in his people? John also shared Alfred's vision of a *Perfecta Saxonia* and identified in the King's grandson Aethelstan, the man who would unite the whole of England. To honour the concept, he wrote a double acrostic hexameter poem to read out at the ceremony in which Alfred nominated Aethelstan as his heir. The acrostic spelt *Adalstan* and the telestich, *Iohannes*—another form of his name, John.

The twenty-sixth day of October, 899, was one of the saddest of my life. King Alfred succumbed to a painful and prolonged illness, one that had troubled him throughout his life. Both John and I hastened to Winchester to attend his burial in the Minster. Five years later, another even more sorrowful event occurred with the death of my oldest and dearest friend, John. Typical of him, he called me to his quarters the evening before his demise. Old and frail, undoubtedly he was but otherwise in reasonable health.

"Prior Gwyn, there is a place not so far from here— Malmesbury, some twenty-five leagues to the north. It is a pretty place where the first saint of Wessex, Saint Aldhelm, had his home. It will be known as the first capital of England. What better place as my final resting place? I beg you to have me interred in the church there. Goodbye, old friend. We will meet in heaven."

"What are you saying? I will see that your wish is fulfilled, but you will live for many more years."

He shook his head, smiled sadly and kissed my cheek. My abbot knew his fate and slipped away in his sleep that same night.

This narrative is not about me, but I am still here. So, to conclude, because my life too is ebbing, King Alfred appointed a new abbot, Seignus, a pious and learned monk who thought fit to retain me as his prior. I am content at Athelney, I have outlived all my friends except Asser, but whenever I consider the new, worthy-enough abbot, I cannot but think that nobody fittingly could fill the sandals of John the Old Saxon.

THE END

APPENDIX

(Verses by Angilbert, who fought the battle -25 June 841 - on the side of Lothar)

Fontenoy they call its fountain, manor to the peasant
known,
There the slaughter, there the ruin, of the blood of
Frankish race;
Plains and forest shiver, shudder; horror wakes the
silent marsh.

Neither dew nor shower nor rainfall yields its freshness
to that field,
Where they fell, the strong men fighting, shrewdest in
the battle's skill,
Father, mother, sister, brother, friends, the dead with
tears have wept.

And this deed of crime accomplished, which I here in
verse have told,

Angibert myself I witnessed, fighting with the
    other men,
I alone of all remaining, in the battle's foremost line.

On the side alike of Louis, on the side of Charles alike,
Lies the field in white enshrouded, in the vestments of
    the dead,
As it lies when birds in autumn settle white off the
    shore.

Woe unto that day of mourning! Never in the round of
    years
Be it numbered in men's annals! Be it banished from all
    mind,
Never gleam of sun shine on it, never dawn its dusk
    awake.

Night it was, a night most bitter, harder than we could
    endure,
When they fell, the brave men fighting, shrewdest in
    the battle's skill,
Father, mother, sister, brother, friends, the dead with
    tears have wept.

Now the wailing, the lamenting, now no longer will I
    tell;
Each, so far as in him lieth, let him stay his weeping
    now;
On their souls may He have mercy, let us pray the Lord
    of all.

———

Translation of acrostic poem by John the Old Saxon. Translator: Gallagher, Robert 2017, Kent Academic Repository.

Behold, may all the graces descend from heaven for you!

You will always be joyful, Alfred, through the happy crossroads [of life].

May you now turn your mind and be satisfied with sacred adornments.

Rightly you teach, hastening away from the deceptive charm of worldly affairs. See, you apply yourself always to gain bright talents,

To run wisely through the fields of foreign learning.

An appeal to readers: please help me out—

I sincerely hope you enjoyed *John the Old Saxon.*

First and foremost, I'm always looking to grow and improve as a writer. It is reassuring to hear what works, as well as to receive constructive feedback on what can be improved. Second, starting out as an unknown author is exceedingly difficult, and Amazon reviews go a long way toward making the journey out of anonymity possible. Please take a few minutes to write an honest review. I would greatly appreciate it.

Best regards,

John Broughton

ABOUT THE AUTHOR

John Broughton was born in Cleethorpes Lincolnshire UK in 1948: just one of many post-war babies. After attending grammar school and studying to the sound of Bob Dylan, he went to Nottingham University and studied Medieval and Modern History (Archaeology subsidiary). The subsidiary course led to one of his greatest academic achievements: tipping the soil content of a wheelbarrow from the summit of a spoil heap on an old lady hobbling past the dig. He did many different jobs while living in Radcliffe-on-Trent, Leamington, Glossop, the Scilly Isles, Puglia and Calabria. They include teaching English and History, managing a Day Care Centre, being a Director of a Trade Institute and teaching university students English. He even tried being a fisherman and a flower picker when he was on St. Agnes island, Scilly. He has lived in Calabria since 1992 where he settled into a long-term job at the University of Calabria teaching English. No doubt his lovely Calabrian wife Maria stopped him being restless. His two kids are grown up now, but he wrote books for them when they were little. Hamish Hamilton and then Thomas Nelson published 6 of these in England in the 1980s. They are now out of print. He's a granddad and, happily, the parents gratifyingly named his grandson Dylan. He decided to take up writing again late in his career. When teaching and working as a translator, you don't really have time for writing. As soon as he stopped the translation work, he resumed writing in 2014.

The fruit of that decision was his first historical novel, *The Purple Thread* followed by *Wyrd of the Wolf*. Both are set in his favourite Anglo-Saxon period. His third and fourth novels, a two-book set, are *Saints and Sinners* and its sequel *Mixed Blessings* set on the cusp of the eighth century in Mercia and Lindsey. A fifth *Sward and Sword* is about the great Earl Godwine. Creativia Publishing has released *Perfecta Saxonia* and *Ulf's Tale* about King Aethelstan and King Cnut's empire respectively. In May 2019, they published *In the Name of the Mother*, a sequel to *Wyrd of the Wolf*. Creativia/Next Chapter also published *Angenga,* a time-travel novel linking the ninth century to the twenty-first. This novel inspired John Broughton's venture, a series of six novels about psychic investigator Jake Conley, whose retrocognition takes him back to Anglo-Saxon times. Next Chapter Publishing scheduled the first of these, *Elfrid's Hole* for publication at the end of October 2019; the second is *Red Horse Vale,* and the third, *Memory of a Falcon*; the fourth is *The Snape Ring*; the fifth, *Pinions of Gold*, the sixth, *The Serpent Wand*, like the others is now on sale at Amazon. The last of the series *The Beast of Exmoor* is also now available.

The author's project previous to *The Rebel Scribes* was a trilogy of 'pure' Anglo-Saxon novels about Saint Cuthbert. The first is *Heaven in a Wild Flower, The Horse-thegn* is the second and the third is *The Master of the Chevron*.

https://www.nextchapter.pub/authors/john-broughton

Printed in Great Britain
by Amazon